GRANDMOTHERS,
INCORPORATED

GRANDMOTHERS, INCORPORATED

A novel by

L. Barnett Evans
and
C.V. Rhodes

CRYSTAL INK Publishing
Indianapolis, Indiana

GRANDMOTHERS, INCORPORATED

Published by CRYSTAL INK Publishing
P.O. Box 53511
Indianapolis, Indiana 46253

Second Edition

ISBN: 0-9719586-2-9

Library of Congress Catalog Card Number: 2004104010

Printed in the United States by Morris Publishing
3212 East Highway 30
Kearney, NE 68847
1-800-650-7888

DEDICATION

This book is dedicated to my mother, Cleo Barnett, who taught me that a youthful spirit is a priceless thing to have; my sister, Nelvia Washington Rent, who is a walking testament to what faith in God can do; and to my sons, Bryant and Preston, who truly are my greatest fans.

L. Barnett Evans

This book is dedicated to the memory of my grandmother, Hattie Williams, whose words of wisdom I still remember; to my mother, Betty Ann Rhodes, my aunts, Virginia Clarke and Florabelle Wilson and to my daughter, Nailah.

C.V. Rhodes

ACKNOWLEDGMENTS

A special thank you to Patricia Shanks and Charles Rent for their help and support, and all the friends and co-workers who were a constant source of encouragement. (LBE)

We would like to extend a warm thank you to Florabelle Wilson, whose editing, suggestions and support has been invaluable. Also, thank you to the multi-talented, Peter Clarke, your great photography made us look very, good. (CVR)

CHAPTER 1

Never in her "sixty-something" years on earth would Beatrice Baker Bell have thought that she would consider sleeping with somebody else's husband. Yet, she was strongly considering it at the moment. Her best friend, Connie, would probably say go for it, while there was no doubt that her other best friend, Hattie, would condemn her to the everlasting fires of hell. Who would have guessed how drastically her life would change in a just a few short weeks, and it all started with the reunion.

Standing in the bedroom of her home on the evening of the event, Bea, as her friends called her, gave a final turn as she checked herself in the mirror before shaking her head in disgust. The black sequined dress just wasn't doing it for her. Taking it off, she tossed it on the bed with the pile of similarly discarded dresses. This evening was special, and she was not about to be the shabbiest dressed woman there. After all, she had a reputation to maintain. She had known and worked with some of the most prominent people in the city of Indianapolis, Indiana, and she had to look the part.

Bea was a stunning five foot, two inches of perpetual motion and constant chatter. With her smooth round face and sparkling dark brown eyes she could pass for a woman half her age—or at least in her forties. She carried her one hundred and fifty-two pound frame with style and sophistication. There had been many male admirers who had given her appreciative looks over the years, especially when she was in high school, and she still managed to turn a few heads. They couldn't help but admire what they saw.

Bea hiked up her slip to get a better look at her shapely legs. On more than one occasion men had referred to her as "that big-legged girl." Her legs were her trademark, and when she was "eighty-something" she knew that they would still look good. Modesty had never been one of her strong points.

Once again, Bea tackled her closet. She had known about the Crispus Attucks High School reunion for over a year. So why wasn't she ready? Maybe her heart wasn't in it as it should be because of the snub from the planning committee. She had applied to be a committee member but had not been chosen. The explanation was that they wanted the last spot to go to an alumnus who resided outside of the capital city. Charlie Mae Crenshaw got her spot. The heifer! That choice had been like rubbing salt in an open wound. After recovering from the shock, Bea had decided that it was their lost. Her influence could have been crucial had they not made *that* mistake, but she wasn't going to let that spoil her evening.

She couldn't wait for tonight. Everyone was going to be there! One of the things that made this occasion so special was the fact that it was an all-school reunion. Every graduate who attended Crispus Attucks High School from its opening in 1927 to its 1986 transition to a middle school had been invited. People still remembered the stir that occurred when the city announced that the high school that had been revered in the city's African American community for decades would be turned into a middle school. What a mess that had been.

Bea sighed. Back to her present situation. She refused to wear some frumpy outfit that did not do tonight's occasion justice. With determination she dove into her closet one more time. High on the shelf, she spotted a long white box that was half-hidden behind a crate full of purses. Squealing with delight she pulled the box down. It was from Strauss Department Store. How many years had it been since that prestigious establishment had closed its doors? That was back in the days when clothes were of high quality. Of course they were expensive, but if they were taken good care of—as Bea had done—they could last forever.

The cream colored, crepe two-piece dress that she pulled from the box was exquisite. As Bea slid it over her shapely hips she muttered a prayer of thanks that it still fit. She could not remember when she had purchased the ensemble, but it looked as though it had been tailor-made for her. The color was perfect, and her olive complexion literally glowed.

As she admired herself in the mirror, Bea glanced at the photo reflected on the four-drawer chest behind her. The picture was of her late husband, James. She smiled. If he were here, he would have given her a flirtatious wolf whistle—his silly way of letting her know when he thought she looked especially nice. They had been married 32 years before his death. That had been a decade ago, and although she had dated many times since then, she had no enthusiasm for entering the confines of marriage again. James had loved her in a quiet and almost fierce way. Yet, her love for him— She glanced away from his picture.

After all of these years, Bea still felt guilty that she had married James on the rebound. In high school Frank Schaffer had been the love of her life. He was, by far, the best-looking boy at school. His voice was a rich baritone timbre that had made Bea physically tremble at its sound. Even at the age of seventeen he had a confidence and determination that attracted attention and demanded respect. She and Frank had dated their junior and senior years in high school. A year after graduation they had announced their wedding plans, but when the wedding was called off Bea was left devastated.

Yet, despite the pain of the past, she couldn't help hoping that Frank would be at the reunion. She looked forward to the possibility of seeing him, just for old time sake.

Yes, tonight was going to be special. She would have a great time finding out what her past classmates had accomplished in their lives. Many graduates of the historic high school had made their mark in the state, the nation and in the world. Among the school's most renowned alumni was basketball great Oscar Robertson, also known as the Big O. It was hoped that he would be at the reunion tonight. Those had been exciting times for the entire city when he played basketball at Attucks. The Mighty Tigers had won two consecutive state basketball championships with the help of the Big O—one in 1955 then again in 1956. The school also won a third championship in 1959.

Bea had been a cheerleader at Attucks and was proud to brag that she could still fit into her cheerleading uniform after all of these years. Of course she couldn't fasten it, but that was okay. She'd had her day.

Noticing the time, Bea frowned. She had better speed things up. She had to pick up her friends Connie Palmer and Hattie Collier. Just as she stepped into her shoes the telephone rang. It was Connie on the other end of the line.

"Hey Bea, I just wanted to see if you're about ready."

"Almost. I'll pick you up at about seven, and then we'll get Hattie."

"That's why I'm calling. I need you to pick me up last."

"Connie, don't fool around and not be ready when I come" Bea demanded.

"Now look here, Bea," Connie countered, "the way you drive I could take a cruise around the world and be ready by the time you get here."

"Girl, don't start talking about my driving, you just be ready." With that, Bea disconnected.

Listening to the dial tone Connie addressed the telephone receiver as though it had spoken to her. "I can't believe that she hung up on me!"

With a nonchalant shrug she dismissed the insult. It wasn't the first time she didn't see eye to eye with Bea and no doubt would not be the last. The important thing was that she now had at least an extra hour before she would be picked up to go to the reunion.

This event was all that Bea and Hattie had been talking about for months. Since Connie wasn't from Indiana and had not attended Crispus Attucks, she didn't quite share their excitement about the occasion, but she was curious about the school and the people who might be attending the evening's event.

From what Connie understood the high schools in Indianapolis had been integrated before the idea of an all

Black institution was introduced in the late 1920's. The proposal was spurred by the political influence of the Klu Klux Klan. Yet, despite the negative reasons that the school had been established, Attucks became a source of great pride in the African American community.

For years Connie had heard her friends brag incessantly about attending Crispus Attucks. Bea and Hattie described their alma mater as the little school that could. They loved the place. They especially loved the Mighty Tigers basketball team. Attucks had been the first school in the city of Indianapolis to win a state championship. Her friends glowed with pride when discussing those days. It almost made her wish that she had gotten the opportunity to attend the school.

Turning her attention to the red satin dress lying on her bed, Connie smiled. She was going to turn some heads tonight! The dress would highlight her pecan brown complexion and certainly flatter her full figure.

Connie weighed in at 200 pounds of voluptuous curves and angles, and if she had to say so herself she wore every pound *very* well. Her late husband, Robert, used to call her "a whole lot of woman." Now that was a man who appreciated a good thing.

Patting her ample chest to make sure that her diamond necklace was still in place, once again Connie grinned at the dress. The men at this reunion had better watch out tonight! Still, bravado aside, she was a little apprehensive about attending the evening's event.

The truth was that Connie had not graduated from high school. When she was Connie Flowers and living in the South, she met, fell in love with and married Robert Palmer. She gave him three sons and a daughter, all healthy and beautiful. Her daughter Earlene had married Bea's oldest son, James, Jr., and they had produced Tina, the granddaughter that she shared with Bea. The girl was Connie's only female grandchild, and she was her heart.

After all of her children had graduated from high school, Connie had studied real estate and joined her husband in his realty business. They made a formidable team. As a result they had become quite wealthy. In anticipation of enjoying that wealth, she and Robert had spent hours planning the leisure activities they would enjoy during their retirement. However, life had altered those plans. Robert's untimely death had squashed those dreams. When she buried her husband, Connie had vowed that she would never again delay living her life to the fullest. She had kept that vow.

She continued to manage the Palmer Real Estate Company alone, adding to her financial wealth. Yet, she still led a relative simple life style. In fact, no one had any idea the extent of her wealth, including her two best friends.

Now fully dressed, Connie picked up the small evening bag that she would be carrying and opened it. The autograph book that she had put there was tucked securely in its place. Good! If basketball great Oscar Robertson was there this evening she planned on getting his autograph. She stepped into her red satin shoes. She was finally ready to go.

Grabbing the telephone she walked down the hallway toward the living room as she dialed Hattie's number. She answered.

"Collier residence."

"Girl! Did Bea call you?"

"Yeah." Hattie put her earrings on, balancing the telephone receiver on her shoulder as she did so. "She told me that you called and said that you wanted to be picked up last."

"That's right."

"Well, just pray that we get to your house alive. You know how she drives. I got Jesus working overtime whenever I get in that car with her." Hattie shuddered thinking about it.

"Well when she gets there, tell her that I'm ready. See you in a few." They disconnected.

Hattie Collier was annoyed. She had figured out exactly how much time she would need to get ready. Now, Bea was picking her up first. Well that was just too bad; she was not going to rush. She wasn't vain, but she wanted to look her best. She had stayed pretty well preserved over the years and welcomed the opportunity to let her old classmates see the results.

Hattie Lou Collier was a very attractive woman. She wore little makeup, just a touch of lipstick, and her dark brown complexion was flawless. Her skin was practically free of age lines. Her delicate face was oval-shaped with full lips and medium brown eyes framed by long lashes. At five feet eight, she was still slender, even after having given birth to two children. The gold colored dress she wore was modest, high necked and long sleeved, but she looked good in it. With one last glance in the mirror Hattie was satisfied with what she saw.

She fluffed her silver-gray hair, aware that the loose bob hairstyle made her look younger than her "sixty-something" years. If she was vain about anything, it was about her hair. It was thick and healthy, soft and silky in texture. She would never wear it in one of those short, nappy Afros like Connie did, or defile it with dye like Bea did hers. A woman's hair was her crown of glory. Her pastor, Reverend Trees, had made the comment that he thought her hair was lovely. Enough said. Her silver gray mane would stay like it was.

Picking up her keys and purse, all she had to do was give Leon a kiss goodbye, and she would be ready to go. Moving from the bedroom to the living room, she walked to the fireplace mantel where her late husband's smiling photograph peered down at her. She and Leon had been married for nearly thirty-five years, and they had never parted without a kiss. Lord, how she missed that man. He had been gone nine years, and she loved him as much today as she did the day she first saw him walking down the hallway of Attucks High School.

She had been a lowly freshman, the daughter of a storefront preacher. Her family was poor and lived by the Canal in a shotgun house. Leon had been a sophomore. His parents were business people. They owned a diner on Indiana Avenue and lived in a nice house on California Street. Tall, dark and handsome described him to perfection. He was totally out of her league, but their love story was a testament that miracles do happen.

She and Leon became a couple, even after Charlie Mae Crenshaw let it be known all over school that she planned on claiming him for herself. However, Leon had other ideas. Her father wouldn't allow Hattie to date, so Leon started attending her father's church and joined the youth choir. Her parents got to know and trust him, and eventually her father gave his approval for him to see his daughter. Leon never betrayed his trust.

She had loved Leon Collier until the day that he drew his last breath. Death had changed nothing. No man would ever take his place.

Hattie took the gold-framed photograph of her husband from the mantel and gave it a kiss goodbye just as Bea honked her horn. Returning the frame to its place of honor, she hurried to the front door prompted by another impatient blast from Bea's horn.

"Beatrice Baker Bell, I wish you'd lay off that darn horn!" Hattie fussed as she slid into the front seat of her friend's midsize sedan.

"Well, come on then. I swear you'll be late to your own funeral."

"Don't you dare swear around me, Bea." Hattie gave a disapproving frown.

"I wasn't swearing, and I plan on having a good time this evening so don't get in with one of those sour puss moods of yours."

Hattie chuckled, drawing a sideward glance from Bea.

"What's so funny?"

"I was thinking about who was really going to have the sour puss mood tonight at the reunion."

"What are you talking about?"

Hattie looked smug. "Guess who I found out headed the reunion planning committee?"

Beatrice looked puzzled. "Evelyn Reynolds headed the committee."

"No, child. Evelyn had a gall bladder operation about six weeks ago, and of course the lazy wench hadn't confirmed any of the arrangements. So the former Charlie Mae Crenshaw stepped in and took over."

"Shut Up!" Bea nearly sideswiped a parked car.

"Lord have mercy!" Hattie squealed. "Watch what you're doing!" Nothing could send Bea up a wall like the mention of Charlie Mae's name.

"That slut!" spat Bea.

The description turned Hattie's momentary fear into laughter. "You just jealous 'cause she stole your boyfriend." She teased.

"Charlie Mae did not *steal* my boyfriend!" Bea retorted. "Frank Schaffer and I had split up before she came along."

"Oh calm down, Bea, I was just pulling your chain. You know I couldn't stand that wench either." But she knew that Bea had even more reason to dislike her.

Frank and Bea had been the couple to envy when they were in high school. They had been so in love and so excited about getting married. He proposed to her graduation night and gave her a ring that was the envy of all of her friends. The two had planned to marry the next year, then suddenly the wedding was postponed.

It turned out that Frank had asked for a delay in their wedding plans, and Bea had raised a ruckus. She wanted to get married on the date *she* had set. Bea worked herself into such a frenzy that she called the wedding off. Frank tried to patch things up between them, but Bea made him suffer a little too long. The next thing everybody knew, Frank had eloped with Charlie Mae.

Hattie never said it verbally, but it was Bea's own fault. She had left Frank out there as bait for a shark like Charlie Mae, knowing darn well that anything in pants wasn't safe around that woman. It was Bea's spoiled, willful ways that had cost her a good man.

Hattie could only imagine what would happen this evening if Bea and Charlie Mae crossed paths. There might be fireworks. They hadn't seen each other in decades, yet their dislike for each other still existed, at least on Bea's part. Hattie had warned Connie about what could occur this evening. Of course the woman had responded to the warning by declaring that if anything did happen she would help Bea kick Charlie Mae's behind—as if *that* were the solution.

Hattie loved Connie like a sister, but the woman had some devilish ways. She had to pray a little harder for her. Connie already had one foot in hell, and the other one was slipping fast.

Bea pulled up in front of Connie's spacious, two story Victorian home located in Indianapolis' historic "Old North Side." Years ago their friend purchased the house for practically nothing, and her girlfriends thought for sure that she was crazy. No one wanted to drive through the neighborhood much less live there at the time. Now the area near downtown was *the* place to live, and the house was worth a fortune. Who knew?

Bea blew the horn. A few moments later Connie appeared. She climbed into the back seat.

"Is everybody ready for this evening?" Her voice held the breathless excitement of facing the unknown.

"Yeah, I'm ready," Bea snapped, pulling off.

Startled by her reaction, Connie gave Hattie a questioning look. She returned the look with one that clearly stated that there was going to be some *mess* tonight.

With a satisfied grin, Connie settled back in her seat. She wasn't sure what was happening, but it looked as though it might be good.

"Ladies, I can't thank both of you enough for inviting me. I can't wait to get to this reunion. Something tells me that this is going to be a night to remember."

CHAPTER 2

A huge "Welcome Attucks Alumni" sign greeted the reunion attendees as Bea, Hattie and Connie entered Crispus Attucks High School. They headed directly to the cafeteria. The room was beautifully decorated with green and gold streamers and balloons. To their astonishment, the women noted that the entire room was painted green and gold. There were nine pillars in the room, each adorned with pictures of distinguished graduates. A lavish soul food buffet had been set up in the front of the room.

"Oh, everything looks so nice!" Connie's eyes took in the entire room as the three women found their reserved table. Her comment included the people as well as the décor.

"I'm surprised that it looks this good, considering Charlie Mae was in charge," Hattie quipped, not willing to give credit whether it was due or not. "That woman never did have any taste."

"Well, there's no arguing that," Bea said begrudgingly, "but I've got to admit, it does look nice in here. So we might as well sit back and enjoy it." They all agreed on that.

The next hour was filled with the joy of greeting old friends and making new ones. Everybody was having a great time when Hattie tapped Connie on the shoulder and pointed across the room. Connie looked over her shoulder, following Hattie's finger. When she saw what she was pointing out, Connie nearly fell out of her chair. Standing near the entrance to the cafeteria was the "Big O" himself! Grabbing her purse, Connie started rifling through it.

"Oh, my Lord! Where is a pen when you need one?"

"What do you need a pen for?" asked Hattie, unaffected by the excitement the celebrity's appearance was causing in the room.

"Are you kidding? That's Oscar Robertson! The man is a legend. I can't leave here without an autograph."

Hattie looked horrified. "Connie Palmer, don't you embarrass me by hassling that man for an autograph. You don't see anybody else trying to get one."

She was right. Despite the stir he was causing, no one had approached him for his signature. Connie meant to change that.

"Fine, Hattie. I just won't tell him I know you." Finding her pen, she hurried across the room.

"That woman acts like Oscar's the only distinguished graduate from this school," Hattie huffed to no one in particular. "There are a lot of distinguished alumni who graduated from Attucks, to say nothing of the faculty."

"You've got that right," Bea grinned. "Remember Dr. John Morton-Finney?"

"Of course." Hattie smiled in remembrance at one of the most respected instructors in Attuck's history. Dr. Morton-Finney had been the first teacher hired at the high school when it opened. "The man was amazing—fluent in six languages and had eleven degrees. Who could forget him?"

Bea nodded as she swallowed the rising lump in her

throat. The pride that she felt in her alma mater and its accomplishments was overwhelming. She had opened her mouth to remind Hattie of another distinguished teacher that she might remember just as an announcement was made for everyone in the crowded cafeteria to move to the auditorium. The talent show was about to begin.

As people filed into the auditorium, the air was charged with excitement. Everyone knew there was no lack of talent among this audience, and those who remembered past talent shows had no reason to believe they would be disappointed with this one. The jovial conversations of the crowd in the auditorium sounded like a swarm of buzzing bees. The audience gradually grew silent as a young man walked out on stage. He lifted a trumpet and played a majestic trumpet call. *Da, da, da, da-a-a. Da, da, da, da-a-a. Da, da, da, da, da, da-a-a.* A disembodied voice came over the PA system.

"Ladies and gentlemen, distinguished alumni and guests. Presenting the chairwoman of this year's Attucks High School reunion, Charmaine Schaffer!

The auditorium went black. Gold and green spotlights danced across the stage and across the audience. On cue, a woman swirled onto the stage in a green and gold floor length gown that complemented her copper complexion. Her chestnut brown hair was piled high on her head. Tiny kiss curls framed her face. The crowd ooh'd and aah'd as she made a theatrical turn in the middle of the stage.

"Well I'll be damned, that's Charlie Mae!" Bea blurted. "Just who does she think she is, Loretta Young or Princess Di?"

Hattie shook her head sympathetically. "It's obvious the woman's lost her mind. She don't even know her name."

Connie leaned toward Bea and Hattie and hissed, "Will you two please be quiet?"

The applause died down, and with exaggerated drama Charlie Mae introduced the Master of Ceremony for the talent show.

"Ladies and Gentlemen, Tigers of all ages . . . I give you Houston Schaffer."

Hattie and Bea applauded enthusiastically in recognition. Houston Schaffer was the younger brother of Frank, Bea's old flame. Although Houston had been several grades below them in school, both women knew him well. He was always tagging after his older brother. For Bea, seeing Houston generated thoughts of Frank. Although not nearly as good looking as his brother, he did resemble him. As he walked across the stage, he seemed to have acquired an easy poise that he had not possessed in the past.

At five feet, ten inches, Houston was shorter than his older brother. In contrast to Frank's smooth cocoa brown skin, Houston's slightly darker complexion, even at fifty something, still held remnants of the acne scars he had suffered with as a youth. He and Frank did share the same warm, brown eyes, but the brothers' personalities had always been different. Frank had been a serious young man with a commanding presence. Houston had been playful, carefree, and sometimes reckless in his undertakings, and while these traits had not always served him well in life, for the moment his vivacious spirit made him the perfect emcee. He was carrying out his duties with humor and gusto.

One by one the performers entertained and excited the crowd. Singers, dancers, jazz and big band musicians, rappers, comedians, and an impressionist all took the stage and captured the audience. For nearly two hours the singing, clapping and toe-tapping shook the auditorium until Houston took the stage to announce the evening's finale.

"And now let's combine generations, old and new school. Are you ready to yell?"

The crowd roared in the affirmative.

"Are you ready to cheer?"

Again, the crowd let out a roar.

"All right, then I want all cheerleaders of Crispus Attucks High School to come up here on stage and lead this crowd in some good old-fashioned cheers."

A buzz went through the auditorium as everyone speculated on what the request meant. Slowly people began to trickle onto the stage while Houston paced the front of the stage with the microphone.

"Now, I know some of us are older, but I don't believe we've turned deaf. I said, I want all former cheerleaders of Cripsus Attucks High School to come up here on stage and lead this crowd in some good old-fashioned cheering. If you were a cheerleader from 1927 through 1986 and can still move, get up here on stage!"

The audience was hyped. The applause was nearly deafening. The stage began to fill as the younger people moved back to make room for the older cheerleaders. Hattie elbowed Bea.

"He's talking about you. Get your behind up there."

"Yes," Connie added. "You're always bragging about how good a cheerleader you were, so show us what you got."

Grinning in response, Bea started to rise from her seat when she saw Charlie Mae come from behind the curtain and work her way toward the front of the stage. Bea and Hattie looked at each other in wide-eyed surprise.

"She wasn't no cheerleader!" Hattie nearly choked on the words.

"Not hardly!!" Bea hissed as she headed down the aisle.

Once on stage, Bea eased into a space beside her friends Dorothy Riggs and Thelma Reeves. Both had been bridesmaids at her wedding. The three of them represented the only cheerleaders from their graduating class. Barely able to control the anger in her voice, Bea turned to Charlie Mae who stood next to her.

"Charlie Mae Crenshaw! Just why are you up here on this stage?"

Charlie Mae looked at her coolly. "I believe the man called for cheerleaders."

"No, what he said was that all *former* cheerleaders of Attucks were to come up here. I didn't hear him say a thing about cheerleader *wanabees*."

Charlie Mae turned to squarely face Bea. "First of all, the name is no longer Charlie Mae. I had it changed to Charmaine."

Bea stepped back in surprise. "You mean like the *toilet paper*?"

"Hell no!" Charlie Mae bellowed. Realizing that she might be heard above the roar of the crowd, she lowered her voice.

"I said *Charmaine*. Secondly, my last name—as you should well know—is Schaffer, or Crenshaw-Schaffer if that will help you remember."

Bea put her hands on her ample hips. "Well, there's one thing you haven't changed. Once a thief always a thief. You stole my man, you stole a product name, and now you trying to steal recognition as a cheerleader."

Charmaine scoffed, "I pity you, Bea. You threw your

man away, and you don't have sense enough to recognize toilet paper from fine linen. After all these years you're still jealous because I could always whip circles around you at everything including cheerleading."

Because the stage was crowded and the audience noisy, no one except Houston and a few others standing closest to them had an inkling of what was being said between the two women, but it was obvious from their body language that warm greetings were not being exchanged. Houston lowered his microphone and stepped between them.

"Ladies, can we please leave our differences aside for one night."

Dorothy spoke up. "Charlie Mae, you know you were *never* a cheerleader. You tried out for the squad twice and was voted down both times, and that's because you weren't any good."

Thelma cut her eyes at Charlie Mae. "The truth is you sucked."

Insulted, Charlie Mae opened her mouth to defend herself, but Houston whispered rapidly in her ear. Nodding, she turned and left the stage reluctantly, throwing Bea, Thelma and Dorothy malevolent looks as she did so. To divert attention from the confrontation, Houston moonwalked to the edge of the stage, delighting the audience.

"All right, you Tigers. We're here because we went to the best high school in this state! We're here because, with the help of some of the most brilliant teachers on earth, this school produced some of the brightest minds in this country, the greatest educators, the best strategic military minds, the most innovative musicians, and everybody in the world knows about our athletes!"

By now the crowd was on its collective feet, cheering, waving and barking its agreement.

"Tigers!" Houston extolled, "Let's give it up for the Attucks cheerleaders!"

As though rehearsed, the different classes stepped up and lead some familiar cheers. The audience followed along as memory served them. When it didn't, they yelled anyway. Someone in the back of the auditorium screamed for "The Crazy Song." The crowd went wild, singing and yelling the song that took Attucks High School to three state basketball championships.

When the last strains of the popular song died and the crowd was a bit more subdued, Houston made a quick announcement of the events planned for the rest of the weekend reunion. There was to be a tour of the Crispus Attucks Museum, a luncheon in the historic Madame C. J. Walker building and the culmination of the event, the Big Prom Bash scheduled for the following evening at the Indiana Roof Ballroom. Connie, Bea and Hattie left the event in high spirits.

As they drove home they recounted the good time had by all, as well as the stage incident with Charlie Mae.

"I can't believe that she came out in public with those kiss curls," Hattie wondered aloud stroking her own silky locks. "What was she thinking?"

"Obviously she wasn't," Connie chuckled. "To tell you the truth, I was looking forward to seeing this good looking husband of hers you all keep talking about. Where was he?" All eyes turned to Bea.

"How should I know?" She sounded defensive. "I haven't seen the man in decades!"

"Well, maybe he'll be at the dance tomorrow night," Hattie said slyly. "If so maybe the two of you can get *reacquainted*."

Bea knew that she was being facetious. "I don't care if

he's there or not. In case you've forgotten, the man's married to the toilet paper queen."

Connie howled with laughter at this reference, while Hattie threw Bea a knowing glance.

"Uh huh, I remember. Just make sure that you do."

* * * *

Bea was trying hard to control her breathing as she stepped into the Indiana Roof Ballroom. She had only been in the fashionable room two or three times in her life, but each time the experience left her breathless. Even the dim lighting could not conceal the exquisite Baroque architecture. The forty-foot dome ceiling created the effect of being under a starry, velvet blue sky. The crescent moon shone down on an array of tables covered in gold linen. Each table held a candle-lit brass lantern surrounded by a bouquet of green and gold flowers. The room's ambiance was magical.

Bea's eyes swept the crowd. As she and her friends moved toward their reserved table, they smiled and nodded at old friends and acquaintances dressed in glittering gowns, elegant suits and tuxedos for the occasion. Some of the men from the graduating classes of the 1970's even managed to find the brightly colored brocade fabric tuxedos from that era. As for Bea, she had outdone herself in dressing for tonight's affair.

She had purchased the deep blue, floor length designer gown she wore months ago on a shopping trip to New York City. It's scooped neckline revealed a generous glimpse of the crowns of her ample breast, and the gathered jacket that covered the dress gave it the appearance of being somewhat modest, that is until she took the jacket off. The dress was backless.

"No you didn't!" Hattie choked as Bea unveiled the creation at their table.

Bea peeked back over her shoulder and gave her a wink. "Yes, I did."

"You go girl!" Connie was delighted. She was dressed in a daring canary yellow designer creation herself.

Bea grinned, grateful for the compliment. She knew that she was looking good. Her hair was in a tight French roll with tear-shaped pearls spaced evenly along the roll. She wore matching tear-shaped pearl earrings in her ears. She was the epitome of elegance and felt it.

The three friends sat back to enjoy the music. It was like taking a stroll through time. Popular tunes from the 40's through the 80's caused squeals of recognition from the crowd. Several men came to the table to ask the three ladies to dance. Bea and Hattie declined, but Connie accepted the invitation from a distinguished looking man. Hattie grumbled as she watched them head for the dance floor.

"Look at that. It's just a sin and a shame the way those people are out there bumping and grinding their way to hell. I've always been against dancing."

Bea raised a questioning brow. "Are you against dancing, or is it that you just can't dance?" She giggled, aware that Hattie had never learned to do so.

"You can laugh all you want, Bea Bell. Getting up and shaking your behind in the face of the world is just a little too much."

"So why did you come tonight? You knew there'd be dancing."

"I came to have a good time with my old classmates. Why do you think? And if I can do the Lord's work by reminding you all why dancing is a sin, so be it."

Bea sighed. There was no point in trying to reason with Hattie. It was time to mingle. She had been glued to this table long enough.

It took her over thirty minutes to stroll the main floor, greeting people from her past and her present and meeting brand new friends. The ballroom was vibrating to the music as a line of dancers crowded onto the floor to do the Electric Slide. Bea burst into laughter when she spotted her friend Dorothy and her husband Nathaniel doggedly trying to keep up with the line of dancers. Connie was out on the floor with another dance partner, and she was having no trouble following the dance moves.

As she made her way up the stairs to the tables in the balcony area, she glanced at the "stars" twinkling from the ceiling and suddenly felt lonely. She wished that James were here to share this moment. Unexpectedly her thoughts flashed to a starry night before she met James—the night that Frank had proposed to her. Startled that her thoughts had betrayed her, she pushed the memory from her mind and continued up the stairway.

In the balcony, tables were placed close to the railing so that occupants could easily see the floor below. There weren't many people up there and none that she recognized, but she continued walking around until she ended up in a section of the balcony just left of the stage. There were no tables in this darkened corner. She was alone, so she stopped to listen to the music. Another band had replaced the previous one and was just about to play. She leaned on the balcony railing to watch as the couples spilled onto the dance floor below and the band struck up a tune.

"It would be a shame to let that great music go to waste."

Bea froze at the sound of the familiar voice.

"Care to dance?"

Slowly she turned to face the only person whose voice could make her quiver inside. In the muted shadows of this deserted area of the balcony she could barely discern the handsome features of the man's cocoa brown face, but she knew every line and plane. She took her time as she raised her eyes to the wide shoulders that filled his tuxedo perfectly, up past the slightly dimpled chin to the dazzling smile.

Frank Shaffer still possessed all of the animal magnetism that Bea remembered. Oh, there were changes. Slight age lines teased the corners of his eyes. His wavy hair was generously sprinkled with gray, as was his mustache. He wasn't quite as muscular as he had been in high school, but it was obvious by his long, lean physique that he worked out to keep his body in the best possible shape. She noticed that his mouth still tilted up at the corners when he smiled, which he did now as she stood flustered by his sudden appearance.

Bea exhaled. She opened her mouth to answer his question, but nothing came out. She was glad, because to shout out "Damn, you look good!" would have left her completely mortified.

Frank chuckled. "I'll take it that the answer to my question is yes." With that he took her hand and in one smooth movement pulled her gently into his arms.

They swayed rhythmically to the band's melodious tones. The section of the balcony where they stood blocked the view of the ballroom's famous ceiling. Gracefully, Frank led them to a more open area where they danced beneath the crescent moon and glittering stars. Bea glanced up at the domed ceiling and was transported back to a time when she was a young girl dancing with the handsomest boy in school. She stopped herself from laying her head on Frank's shoulder, reminding herself that he had not only been the love of her life but he was the man who had practically left her at the altar. *This is also the man who was married to Charlie Mae Crenshaw!* The last thought sobered her like a slap in the face.

As the last notes of the brass section faded, she firmly extracted herself from Frank's embrace and took a step backward. His eyes scorched her from her head to her feet.

"How are you, Bea? You look beautiful. You have no idea how great it is to see you again."

"It's good to see you, too, Frank." She was formal. "Thank you for the compliment. You're looking pretty good yourself."

An awkward silence followed, but his smile continued to warm her. Bea could feel her face become flush. She dropped her eyes, no longer able to hold his gaze. Frank spoke.

"I'm sorry. I don't mean to stare, but I can't get over how little you've changed. The same eyes." He brushed a fingertip down her cheek. "The same soft, lovely skin."

To cover her discomfort, Bea changed the subject. "I've heard through the grapevine that you're doing fine. Your realty company is thriving. The talk here is that you and Charlie Mae are very happy and doing well."

"Really?" He looked surprised. "That's interesting, but let's not talk about me. I heard about your husband's death years ago. I wanted to call with my condolences, then thought it best that I didn't." He paused, knowing that she understood the reason why, and she did. He continued. "I trust that your children are doing well."

"Bryant is doing quite well. He's a police officer here in Indianapolis." Bea hesitated, then added, "My son, James Jr., died about three years ago."

"Your son? Dead? I had no idea! I'm sorry. Charmaine and I never had children so I can't imagine what it must be like to lose one."

Frank took both her hands in his. His look of sympathy was so sincere that Bea had to resist bursting into tears.

"Thank you, Frank." Struggling to maintain control of her emotions, she cleared her throat and once again changed the subject. "You know, for a second there I had no idea who the woman named Charmaine was. I mean *Charlie Mae*."

"Okay, Bea, don't start." Frank gave her a warning look.

She feigned innocence. "What? I'm trying to be nice and dispel what they say about a woman scorned."

"Scorned?" Frank was incredulous. "You're saying *that's* what happened?" He shook his head. "I know about women scorned, but ones with selective memories are a different matter."

Bea was taken aback. *Selective memory! She ought to knock his lights out.*

"Bea, it's been too many years, and it's been too good seeing you, so let's not fight. I only had two reasons to come to this reunion. The first one I can't even remember, but the second one was to see you."

Bea's heart skipped a beat, but before she could respond she caught a movement out of the corner of her eye. The dim lights in the balcony couldn't disguise Charlie Mae's looming presence.

"So there you are, Frank. Someone said that they saw you come in. I've been looking everywhere. People have been asking for you." She turned to Bea with a chilly smile.

"You don't mind do you? I need to *steal* my husband from you." Charlie Mae looked at Bea pointedly.

Before Bea could retort, Charlie Mae looped her arm through Frank's and tried to pull him away. He resisted. Ignoring his wife he turned back to Bea.

"It's great seeing you again, Bea, and I *will* get back with you later."

Bea watched as Frank and Charlie Mae walked away. It felt like *deja vu.*

CHAPTER 3

"You are gonna burn in hell!" Hattie declared fervently. She was right on her heels as Bea hurried down the stairway. The woman was getting on her last nerve.

Hattie had been so concerned by Bea's dinner date this evening that she had taken a city bus to her house. The purpose, as she explained, was to "save her from Satan."

Frank Schaffer had called Bea from Ft. Wayne to inform her that he would be in Indianapolis on business today. He asked if he could see her. It had been weeks since the reunion, and they had made numerous telephone calls to each other since then, calls that she told herself were harmless. Their conversations had often been no more than brief chitchat or a word of hello, but each time that she heard his voice, her heart skipped a beat. Today it was beating out of control. She was going to see him again. She had never shared their calls or her feelings with her friends, but unfortunately, this friend had managed to find out more than she wanted her to know.

"The man is married, Bea, but that doesn't seem to be bothering you a bit." Hattie followed her down the stairs, determined to save her friend's soul.

Bea wanted to tell her that his marital status had

crossed her mind, but only briefly. Most of her thoughts had been about Frank, not Charlie Mae. Since the reunion she hadn't been able to think of much else. How was it possible that her feelings for a man that she hadn't seen in decades could still be so strong? Life had been good to them both since their parting. It wasn't as if time had stood still. Yet, when she first saw him again it seemed as though it had. Why did Hattie have to make such an issue about this evening? It was simply two old friends sharing a meal together, nothing more.

Bea had nobody to blame but herself for Hattie having caught wind of this evening's appointment. The two of them shared the same beautician, Big Mouth Roberta Hamon.

Earlier this morning, Bea had begged Roberta to squeeze her in for an appointment. She had made the mistake of letting it slip that she had a "dinner *date* with a friend tonight," and that was why she was so desperate. Of course the woman complied. Bea gave no names, even after Roberta got her in the chair and interrogated her as if she were an enemy spy. Hattie had gone to Roberta later for her regular appointment, and of course the woman blabbed Bea's business. Hattie called her on her cell phone from the beauty shop trying to get into her private affairs. Even then, Bea remained noncommittal.

Ever relentless, the nosey woman named everybody they both had known since the beginning of time in an effort to guess the "dinner date" possibilities, but to no avail. Bea wasn't talking.

"Come on," Hattie whined, frustrated. "I don't know what the big deal is. Shoot, you'd think that you were stepping out with a married man or something." It took two seconds to realize that she had hit the jackpot. "I *know* that you're not going out with Frank Shaffer!" She croaked the words like a frog in shock.

Bea remained silent, just as she had through all of the other guesses, but it didn't fool her. Hattie had hit pay dirt, and she knew it. She later claimed that it was the Lord helping her sniff out sinners.

"Sweet, Jesus! You stay where you are. Don't go anywhere," she demanded. An hour later she was at Bea's front door ringing the buzzer. She started not to let her in.

As Bea took her wrap from the hall closet, she wished that she had left Hattie's butt standing on the front porch. The woman was a pest.

"You're no better than a Jezebel if you do this," Hattie declared in her fervor to get her best friend to change her mind.

Tired of her jabbering, Bea whirled on her. "It's just dinner, Hattie, two people breaking bread together. It's not a roll in the hay, so back off!" She felt like smacking her.

"Humph! Tell that to Satan cause I ain't buying it!" Hattie cast a skeptical eye on the body slimming dress that Bea wore. It was sky blue, her friend's favorite color. If she remembered correctly it used to be Frank's favorite color too.

"You better listen to me, Bea. You and that man are reserving your spaces in the eternal flames with this flirtation."

"Let's go!" Bea barked, snatching her purse from the table. "I'm taking you home." She headed toward the front door. Hattie was hot on her heels.

"You better do some hard thinking about this, my friend. Charlie Mae would be justified in coming down here and kicking your behind. You better watch out."

Bea unlocked the passenger door, then turned narrowed eyes to Hattie. "I haven't *done* anything! But I'm going to do you a favor and take you home, but I'm warning you, if you say one more word to me I'll pull over and throw you out, no matter where we are. So, you'd better keep your mouth shut all the way to your house."

Hattie glared back at her, but got into the car without a word. As Bea pulled off she hoped that the silence would continue. She didn't have a problem with what Hattie was saying. She was familiar with her sermonizing. What bothered Bea was how close she was to the truth. Never in her life would she have thought that she would entertain the possibility of doing *anything* with a married man. Yet, she was thinking about it—*hard*.

When Frank asked her to dinner she hadn't hesitated, but she did insist on meeting him at the restaurant. That eliminated the possibility of him coming to her house under any circumstances. She didn't want to take the chance that if he brought her home she would be tempted to do something that she might regret. She was already nervous enough about this evening. She didn't want something else to worry about, and she certainly didn't need Hattie's opinion on the matter. It was only making things worse.

Afraid to test Bea's resolve, a tight-jawed Hattie was silent during the ride home. When they pulled up to her house, she gave Bea a malicious glare before climbing from the car.

"Just because Charlie Mae is a cow don't mean that you have to ride her bull."

Shutting the car door behind her, Hattie gave a triumphant smile as an angry Bea skidded away from the curb.

* * * *

Bea's stomach was in knots by the time she arrived at the restaurant where she was to meet Frank. Located at the top of a downtown hotel, the revolving restaurant offered a panoramic view of the city below as it rotated 360 degrees. Stepping off the elevator she could hardly enjoy her surroundings. Hattie's tongue-lashing had upset her so badly. She arrived a few seconds before Frank which gave her a little time to pull herself together, but she had barely done so when she turned to see the doors of the elevator open and Frank exit. He looked so good that for a moment Bea's breath caught in her throat.

He had always been stylish in his dress, and this evening was no different. His expensive pin-striped suit fit his still slender frame to perfection. The snow-white shirt he wore complemented his rich cocoa brown complexion as did the red tie with matching handkerchief tucked neatly in the jacket pocket. Bea swallowed hard. It was a sin and a shame for a man in his sixties to look this good. She steeled herself to act as normal as possible as he walked toward her with that smooth gait that she remembered so fondly.

"Well, hello." His dark eyes sparkled with pleasure.

"Hi," Bea muttered, suddenly shy. She stuck her hand out to shake his, and he laughed.

"You're kidding, aren't you?" Frank leaned down and placed a kiss near her ear. She wondered if he still remembered that was her favorite spot. At least *one* of them.

Stepping back, he took both of her hands in his and gave her a long, slow perusal from head to toe.

"It's so nice seeing you again, Bea. You look good." He nodded his approval. "Real good."

"Thanks." She felt like an idiot. Surely her vocabulary consisted of more than one word at a time. Clasping her elbow he moved them toward the hostess.

"Let's get our table."

As he spoke to the hostess, Bea felt like a giddy schoolgirl standing beside him. The hostess showed them to a table by the window. She hardly remembered the walk across the room or being seated because the intoxicating scent of Frank's after-shave had dulled her senses. Silently she prayed that she could get through dinner with some semblance of dignity. It had been a long time since she had enjoyed the company of a man. She felt highly susceptible. Perhaps Hattie had been right. Maybe this had been a bad idea. Talking to him on the telephone was one thing, but being here with him in the flesh was more than her senses could take. Her hands were shaking so badly that she placed them in her lap.

The solicitous waiter was at their table as soon as they were seated. Frank asked her drink preference, and she went brain dead. All she could think of was water. He ordered a glass of white wine for himself. When the waiter left Frank leaned back in his seat and flashed a warm smile.

"Do you know how long it's been since I've sat across a dinner table from you?"

"Too long," Bea answered, glad that her vocabulary had worked its way up to two words.

"I agree." Crossing his arms, Frank leaned across the table and gave her a smile so sensuous that Bea thought that she would melt right out of her drawers. "I know that you won't believe this, but I've missed you all of that time."

Bea chuckled. She might be nervous, but she wasn't crazy. "Sure you did, Frank. You missed me so much that you up and married another woman not long after we broke up."

His smile vanished. He leaned back in his chair. "*Broke* is the operative word, because that's what you did to my heart when you left me, and up to this very day I never understood why you did it."

It was funny, but Bea couldn't remember why she did it either. No disrespect to her late husband, but Frank was the best thing that had ever happened to her. She had really loved the man. There had been passion between them, something that she had never found with James. It was the same undercurrent of passion that had simmered between them at the reunion, the same one that was brewing now. Frank continued.

"All I asked was that we postpone the wedding for a couple of months."

"But you never told me why. I deserved an explanation at least."

"I did tell you it was something that had to do with my brother, Houston."

"Yes, but you weren't specific. All I know is that you used our wedding money to get him out of some sort of trouble."

"But I thought you would trust me enough that details wouldn't be necessary."

"And *I* thought that you loved me enough to put me first."

Frank sighed in frustration. "Houston is family, Bea."

Recognizing that their disagreement was escalating, she redirected the conversation.

"Let's talk about something more pleasant, Frank. What kind of business brings you to town?"

Frank studied her for a moment. "So you don't want

to talk about this anymore. All right, you've got the right to reserve that privilege." He sounded disappointed. "As for your question, I had a meeting with a local attorney to go over some information that I discovered, and if it's true, it's going to keep me from losing a fortune." He patted his jacket pocket, then sighed. "My other reason for being here, unfortunately, is a sad one. A colleague of mine died unexpectedly."

"Oh, I'm sorry."

The waiter interrupted them as he returned with salads and their drinks. Placing them on the table he slipped away quietly.

"He died of a stroke," Frank continued. "They buried him today. Or maybe I should say that they disposed of his body."

"Oh really? What does that mean?"

"He was cremated."

"You're kidding!"

"They had him in an urn. I had expected a body and a casket, but all that was left of him was ashes."

"Hmmmm," Bea didn't know what to say about that. She didn't know anybody in her crowd who wanted their body burned instead of buried after they died. She thought that sort of thing was kind of sacrilegious, but—

"The bible does say ashes to ashes, dust to dust." She took a sip of water. Her initial uneasiness had begun to wane.

"I know, but when I die I want my whole body to rot *slowly.*"

Bea laughed. She had forgotten what a sense of humor he had.

"But seriously, I don't want anybody burning me up when I'm dead." He and Bea both chuckled at his description of the scenario.

"I know what you mean," she grinned at him across the table, enjoying his company more and more. "I just don't understand why people do that kind of thing."

"Me neither," Frank admitted. "All I know is that I've left instructions that when my time comes I want to be put in the ground *intact*!"

Bea lifted her water glass. "I'll toast to that." They tapped glasses.

The waiter appeared with their dinner plates. As he served them with the efficiency of a pro, Bea kept her eyes downcast aware that Frank's gaze was riveted on her. It was as if he could look straight into her heart. She felt exposed, and at this moment very confused. She didn't want to have lingering feelings for Frank. What had happened between them had been long ago. It should have been forgotten by now, but it hadn't been. How could it? He had been her first love—her first lover—and it seemed that time had only served to dim the memory of how they once felt for each other, not extinguish the flame.

Completing his task the waiter faded away. Bea raised her eyes to find Frank's eyes waiting for her. Time didn't seem to matter where they were concerned. *Yet*, there was one thing that did matter, very much.

"You're married, Frank." The statement needed no preface.

"Not for long." He continued to hold her eyes. "I'm getting a divorce."

The wind sucked from Bea's lungs. "That's the oldest line in the world." *Was it possible?*

"I could debate that. I think that 'I love you' is the world's oldest line." There was a pregnant pause. He searched her face for a reaction. She gave him none. He continued. "The truth is that Charmaine and I haven't been living as man and wife for years. We even sleep in separate bedrooms."

Bea gasped in surprise at the revelation. "That's a little too much information." She took a sip of water.

Frank didn't smile at the quip. His manner was serious. "We should have divorced a long time ago. It took a while for us to realize what a mistake our marriage had been."

"Decades?" A hint of sarcastic cynicism was in Bea's tone. Frank nodded.

"You're right. It continued for *too many* decades. What I thought was love turned into convenience, then greed took a hold. Eventually that deteriorated into loathing. Believe me, it's not a pleasant way to live. There's nothing worse than being in an unhappy marriage, except letting it continue for too long."

"Is that why you never had children?"

"Why bring an innocent life into a chaotic situation. Over the years I asked Charmaine for a divorce numerous times, but she refused."

"You could have filed." She wasn't going to make this easy for the man who had broken her young heart.

"That's where the greed comes in. The assets we own—and that's substantial—are in both our names. I guess that I wasn't miserable enough to sacrifice giving up everything that I worked so hard to get. But the tide has turned." He patted the same breast pocket that he had indicated earlier. "As the kids say, I've got a little something, something that's going to turn things in my favor. Plus, I'm tired, Bea. I'm sick and tired of living a lie." He started eating his dinner, silently closing the topic of conversation.

Bea didn't push for further information. On some

level she could empathize with Frank. She had not been in love with her husband when she married him, but she had grown to love him. She had married James on the rebound behind what she perceived as Frank's betrayal. At the time she told herself that she hated Frank and would never forgive him. Time seemed to have proved that declaration false.

As they sat enjoying their dinner and exchanging conversation about mundane things, Bea couldn't help but feel a bit of satisfaction that Frank and Charlie Mae had been miserable in their marriage. It might not be Christian of her, but as far as she was concerned, it served them both right.

As the evening progressed, Bea relaxed and enjoyed Frank's company. The restaurant in which they were dining was known as the most romantic in the city. The soft candlelight all around them, the glowing street lights below them and the twinkling stars in the sky above them added ambiance to the evening. Everything was perfect. She and Frank laughed and talked about old times at Attucks, carefully avoiding any mention of their relationship, but the magic of their former union was in the back of both of their minds.

They were happy to be together again. It was reminiscent of old times when they were young and in love and the whole world was wonderful. Back then their future looked bright. Yet, those memories were dangerous and could forge visions of nights filled with unquenchable passion—nights better forgotten. They needed very little to raise the heat simmering between them to the boiling point. It was already close to that now.

Bea declined dessert, but they did linger over coffee, both reluctant to call it an evening, but the night had to end. It was late. They were the last diners to leave the restaurant.

As they rode the glass elevator down to the lobby, the blood racing through Bea's veins flowed as rapidly as the waterfall paralleling their descent. Alone with him in the confined space, she was aware of every breath Frank took. Never had she been more attuned to another human being. By the time they reached the lobby and proceeded outside, she had to will herself to put one foot in front of the other.

They were standing side by side outside the hotel in the warm night air waiting for the valets to deliver their cars when Frank turned to her.

"I'm going to follow you home. It's too dangerous for you to be out this time of night alone."

"I've been out later than this alone," Bea protested. "I'll be okay."

Frank's car pulled up, and a split second later Bea's car pulled up behind it. He helped her into her car and closed the door. She rolled the window down, praying silently that he wouldn't repeat his offer to follow her home.

"I want to thank you for a lovely evening, Frank. I really enjoyed it."

He leaned down to address her, offering another delicious whiff of his cologne.

"You're very welcome, but the night isn't over. Like I said, I'm following you home."

Once again Bea opened her mouth to protest, but he had already walked away. She moaned. "Lord, help me."

She would need all of the assistance that she could get. If Frank got out of his car to walk her to the door, it would take all of the strength that she could muster to make sure that she entered her house alone. The man was much too tempting.

Never in her "sixty-something" years on earth would Bea have thought that she would consider sleeping with somebody else's husband. Yet, this was the dilemma that she found herself in at the moment as she strongly considered the possibility. All the way home she fretted and worried. Perhaps after seeing that she had arrived safely at her house, Frank would drive away, eliminating the temptation. She pulled into her driveway. No such luck. He pulled in behind her and parked his car.

Bea walked stiffly beside him as they headed toward her front porch. Although she tried to appear calm, she was certain that he could hear the beat of her heart. The heat generating between them had intensified. She broke into the kind of sweat that she hadn't experienced since going through the change. The key in her hand shook as she tried to insert it into the keyhole. Gently, Frank took the key from her hand and unlocked the door in one movement. He handed it back to Bea.

"Thank you." Her voice was an unsteady whisper.

"You're welcome." Frank took a single step toward her. His eyes were ablaze.

Bea inhaled. He was entirely too close for comfort. How could he appear so cool, calm and collected when she was about to fall apart? She had been nineteen years old when she last felt like this.

"Uh, like I said, uh, I . . . I enjoyed myself this evening." *What was wrong with her? She was stuttering like an idiot!*

"Bea." Frank stepped closer. As if hypnotized, she swayed toward him.

Years ago they did forbidden things that could have

led to complications in their lives from which they might never have recovered, but it didn't matter to them then. One touch, one kiss was all it took to toss them into a sea of desire.

"Bea." He reached out and drew her to him. His breathing was erratic.

As he lowered his face, and his lips caressed her temple, Bea told herself emphatically that what she was about to do was wrong. It could lead to difficulties that she didn't want or need, but when he placed a soft kiss on that special place near her ear. She closed her eyes, and rationale disappeared until—*Ring!*

Bea's eyes flew open. *What in the world?* Frank took a step back. They looked at each other in bewilderment, and then at the small handbag hanging from her arm. *Ring!* It was her cell phone.

Frank frowned. "I guess you'd better get that. It might be an emergency."

Bea could feel the heat of embarrassment replace the heat of desire. She fumbled for the clasp on her purse. "I'm so sorry. I didn't know that it was on."

Groping for the small telephone inside the bag, she withdrew it, unable to mask her anger at whoever had disturbed the special moment. She glanced at the caller ID. It was Hattie calling.

Bea sighed. "Hello."

"Have you sinned yet?" Obviously a polite greeting wasn't an option.

"I'm home safely." Bea glanced up at Frank with a weak smile. "Let me call you back." She disconnected without waiting for a reply. She made sure that the telephone was turned off this time.

Taking a deep breath, Bea stuck out a trembling hand.

"I had a wonderful time this evening. It was unforgettable. Thank you."

Hesitating, he looked from Bea to her outstretched hand then back at her. The slightest of smiles crossed his face. His eyes reflected resignation. Taking her hand he turned it over and placed a kiss in her palm. It sent shock waves clear to her toes.

"Goodnight, Bea. I had a wonderful time too."

Turning, he walked down the porch steps as she opened the door and stepped inside.

"Bea?" His voice halted her in the doorway. She turned to him.

"Yes?"

"I'll be calling you, because this is only goodnight, not goodbye."

She watched from the doorway as he got into his car and drove away into the night. It took everything not to call him back to her as his declaration echoed in her head. *This is only goodnight, not goodbye.*

The shrill ring of the telephone in the living room interrupted her errant thoughts. As she moved to answer it, she knew who it was. Her personal voice of conscience was calling again, and just in the nick of time.

CHAPTER 4

Hattie woke up with a pounding headache. The night before she had again tried to talk Bea out of her sinful ways. She knew it would happen. Bea and Frank hadn't ended their communication with the dinner they had several weeks ago. They weren't kids anymore, and Hattie was sure that dinner and a few telephone conversations were not all that they planned on sharing. But she was Bea's friend, not her mother. If the woman wanted to burn in hell over another woman's husband, so be it. Besides those two were only half her headache. Hattie had an important decision she had to make.

She made her way through the house opening curtains and checking to see that nothing had been disturbed during the night. She checked every morning to see if things were out of place. She knew it was foolish. There was no one else living in the house to move anything. The only person rattling around in this big house was her. She only wished that . . . Hattie froze in place.

Okay, stop right there, sister. Don't you dare show ingratitude after all the Lord has done for you. Michael and Cynthia are two of your greatest blessings, and their children—your grandchildren—are the joy of your life. It's just that sometimes it's so hard going to bed alone.

Walking over to the mantle, Hattie stood in front of the photograph of her late husband. As was her morning and evening ritual, she kissed his picture.

"You know I'm faithful to you, Leon, but it gets hard. I miss you so much." Hattie sighed and headed for the kitchen. She had the same breakfast nearly every morning, one scrambled egg, one piece of toast, a bowl of oatmeal and a cup of hot tea. As she absentmindedly reached in the cabinet for a bowl, she knocked over an open box of salt.

"A pinch of salt to save a pound of pain," she said. Taking a pinch of the salt she threw it over her left shoulder. She felt a guilty relief that her children were not there to witness the moment. They were forever scolding her about her superstitions, but better safe than sorry.

Hattie sat down to eat her breakfast, slowly savoring every morsel. She read the newspaper as she ate. Every article including the sports page and classified ads were read before she turned her attention to the obituary column. Hattie's eyes fell on the name Emma Sanders, a fifty-seven year old woman who had died in a car accident five days earlier. The Sanders woman's funeral was today at three o'clock. She had no plans around that time, so she made a mental note to find something to wear to the funeral. The Sanders woman was a total stranger, but according to the article she belonged to the Baptist church barely six blocks from where Hattie's son, Michael, attended. That was practically the same as knowing her. Besides, since the obituary made no mention of family, someone had to mourn the poor woman. It was her Christian duty to be at that funeral.

Her children often teased her about being a professional mourner, but that just showed how ignorant they were. Wouldn't they want someone to come to their funerals? Well, she sure wanted someone to be at her last rites, so she figured that by attending other people's funerals she was guaranteed that somebody would return the gesture.

Hattie checked the time. It was ten o'clock and probably a little early to call Reverend Trees, but something was weighing on her mind. She had to get some answers. She wasn't sure that Connie and Bea would understand, so she ruled out talking to either of them. Naturally, she thought of the church as the next place to seek an answer.

Hattie was one of the founding members of her church. She had been there eighteen years ago when Reverend Trees was appointed pastor. She had been impressed with him from the beginning. Over the years she had come to know him as a true man of God. His confident knowledge of God's word impressed her. She tried not to focus on his physical appearance, and that was difficult. He was a fine specimen of a man. He was a little small in stature—only five feet, eight inches tall—but fit. He was a man who took care of himself physically. His shock of wiry silver hair always seemed to need combing, and his bushy black eyebrows at times gave him a sinister look. When she allowed herself to think about such things, Hattie had to admit that his best feature was his booming bass voice that commanded attention even when he was speaking in moderate tones. She also liked his strong hands. Many times those hands had helped the missionary sisters carry supplies to nursing homes and hospitals, lifted young children from their mother's arms to give warm kisses, welcomed the newly saved into the church fold and supported the arm of ladies to help them into the church van. Yes, he had strong hands.

Hattie halted her mental musing when she thought of Leon's picture resting on the mantel in the other room. Quickly she began to busy herself clearing the kitchen table. Another half-hour passed before she called the pastor's office.

"Good morning, Reverend Trees speaking." His voice rumbled through the receiver.

"Good morning, Reverend. This is Hattie Collier."

"Sister Collier! It's so good to hear from you." With concern in his voice he added, "How is everything? Are your children okay? The grandchildren? Your voice sounds a little strained?"

"No, Reverend, my family is fine, thank you for asking, but there is something I need to talk with you about."

"Is something wrong with *you*, Hattie?" The reverend's tone softened. "I mean, Sister Collier?"

His inquiry was so sincere that Hattie was alternately pleased and embarrassed.

"I-I'm fine, Reverend. It's about my mother-in-law, Fanny Collier. Remember I told you that she said that she wasn't feeling especially well, and was concerned with living by herself?"

"Yes, Sister Collier, I remember that we talked about it briefly."

"Well, she's done it. She's actually come out and asked me if she could move in with me. I know it's not the Christian thing to do, but I'm desperate to come up with some reason why she can't. First of all, there is nothing wrong with her. Second, she's a nosey busybody, and she just plain gets on my nerves."

Hattie paused to see if the reverend would offer some comment, but when he didn't she hurried on.

"Have you ever watched that t.v. show where the mother is always barging in on her son who lives across the street? What is the name of that show? Anyway, she criticizes the wife's cooking, the way she cleans house, and the way she raises the kids. That show might as well have been about Fanny Collier."

Hattie stopped to take a breath and calm down. Reverend Trees used the lull in the conversation to address her in his most pastoral voice.

"How old is Miss Fanny?"

"She's eighty-something." Hattie wondered what that had to do with anything.

"She's an old lady who doesn't want to spend her last years alone, and even though her son is dead you're still family. Now ask yourself, Sister Hattie, what would Jesus do?"

"Well I ain't Jesus, Reverend, but I suppose you have a point. I do want to do right by Leon's mother."

"I'm not saying you should or shouldn't move her in. I'm just saying to weigh things in your mind. I know you'll do what's right."

"Reverend, I sure do appreciate you taking time to talk with me."

"Sister Collier, it's always a pleasure to talk to you. My door is open to my flock, and *you're* welcome to call me anytime."

There was an awkward moment of silence, and finally the reverend said, "Are you planning to go with us next week for the prison ministry? We meet at the prison on Thursday, now."

"Yes, Reverend, I'll be there." Hattie could sense his pleasure at her answer. "Thanks again."

After hanging up, Hattie gloomily rehashed his words. She supposed that it was her Christian duty to take in the woman. After all, Miss Fanny *was* Leon's mother and the grandmother of their two children. Maybe this was a test from the Lord. Surely there was a blessing in it for taking in that mouthy woman. In fact, the more she thought about it, the more certain Hattie was that the Lord *was* testing her, and she was determined to pass with flying colors. She did have room for her, and the woman had money of her own to support herself. *I guess if I don't kill her, it will work out.*

Hattie started at this last thought, then scolding herself for thinking such a thing she hurried to get ready for the funeral service. She wanted to catch the bus on time. Quickly she bathed and fixed her hair. There was not much need to search for something to wear. She had a lovely, plain black dress that she wore on such occasions. She added tiny pearl earrings and a matching necklace to accessorize the dress, then looked in the mirror. Satisfied that she would do Emma Sanders justice as one of her mourners, she got her purse and began to count out change for the bus.

Hattie was headed for the door when the telephone rang. She looked at the clock trying to decide whether she should answer it. She had never learned to ignore a ringing telephone. So, even though she might be late for the funeral service, she answered the insistent ringing.

"Hello."

* * * *

Connie Palmer put down the book she had been reading. She wanted to get ready for her appointment. In a couple of hours she was scheduled to close on a house she had recently purchased, and she could hardly wait. Signing on the dotted line gave her such a feeling of satisfaction. She loved dealing in real estate. In the near future she envisioned starting a school that trained people in the real estate business. She wanted the endeavor to be affordable to single mothers who needed a decent income to take care of their families. She hadn't shared this dream with her family or with her friends, but there were a lot of things she hadn't shared with them.

Climbing the stairs, Connie waved her hand over an electronic beam that raised the glass door to her bedroom—just one of the unusual features of her home. A sensual smile creased her face as her eyes glided to the figure lying between the rumpled sheets on her bed. There was something else she hadn't shared with her friends and family.

Stealing quietly across the room so that she wouldn't disturb the sleeping figure, Connie headed for the bathroom to take a shower, veering to her spacious closet on the way. She had to find something to wear to her appointment. As she concentrated on her task she didn't hear the stealthy steps behind her. Turning, she gave a startled yelp as she bumped into the solid chest of her little secret.

The man standing before her was not only tall and muscular, but he was also fifteen years her junior. His dark brown eyes traveled over her body covered by the silk robe she wore. He crossed muscled arms that attested to not only many hours of manual labor, but to just as many hours spent in a gym. As if by instinct, Connie pulled her robe together more as a shield rather than a cover. Gently, he pried the robe open again and slid it down her body then tossed it aside.

"Don't do that. Don't hide your body." He smiled revealing rows of even, white teeth. "I like what I see."

Pleased by his compliment but still embarrassed, Connie swatted his arm feigning annoyance.

"Boy, you scared me!"

"Boy? Oh, I got your boy," he growled bringing her to him in a vice-like grip.

Connie struggled halfheartedly for a moment, but her resistance waned as his lips met hers. The kiss grew deeper and more passionate before coming to a slow, satisfying end.

"David," Connie whispered behind a contented sigh.

She had met David Austin several years ago when she hired him to manage her property. They worked together closely on the renovation of two of her houses, and it wasn't long before their friendship developed into a love affair. The age difference between them wasn't an issue. Connie was never one to stand on convention. As she snuggled in his arms and relished his kisses she recognized that she wanted him as much as he seemed to want her. She was glad that they had started their affair, but she didn't see the need to share this relationship with anyone—not yet. The jangle of the telephone distracted them both.

"Don't answer it," David whispered, nipping at her ear.

"It might be important." Connie ignored his groan of displeasure as she went to the bedroom and answered the telephone on the nightstand.

"Hello?"

"Connie, it's Hattie. I've got Bea on the other line. She's crying so hard I can barely make out what she's saying, but she wanted to do a three-way."

Anxious, Connie sat down on the bed as Hattie made the connection.

"Hello, Bea. It's Connie."

Hattie was right. Bea was sobbing uncontrollably. "H . . . h . . . he's gone. Oh my God, he's gone!"

Connie's concern escalated. "Bea, what is it? What's wrong?"

"What's happened?" asked Hattie. "Who's gone?"

"Frank! He's gone!"

Both women were confused. Hattie spoke up. "You mean gone like left you? What are you talking about?"

"I . . . I called his office and . . . and his secretary answered, and she . . . she said that he . . . he . . . "

"He what?" Connie prodded impatiently.

"He's gone. Frank Schaffer is dead!"

CHAPTER 5

"I sure hope that I live to be seventy-something." Hattie sat in the back seat of Bea's car with her arms folded and her lips pursed. "I swan it, Bea, I may not know how to drive, but I do know that riding with you is like roller skating on the freeway. It's a sure-fire way to reach heaven early."

"You're live until God calls you home," Bea snapped, annoyed at Hattie's customary back seat driving. She moved across the center line that she had been straddling back into her lane. "I don't know why they don't paint these blasted lines in iridescent colors so people can see them."

The three ladies were headed up Interstate 69 on their way to Fort Wayne, Indiana to attend Frank Shaffer's funeral. Bea had been hell bent on going to the sad affair. Nothing could stop her. She had taken the news of Frank's death hard. Hattie noted that Bea had experienced a lot of grief over the past few years—first her husband, then her son, and now this. Her heart went out to her. Yet, Hattie still suspected that some hanky panky might have been going on between Bea and Frank.

Neither one of Bea's friends would allow her to go to Fort Wayne by herself. They insisted that they come along just in case Charlie Mae acted a fool. If so, they would be there to have Bea's back.

"Are you sure we're headed right, Connie?" Bea took her eyes off the road briefly to glance at her. Connie had been designated as the navigator, but Bea wasn't quite sure of her map reading skills.

Irritated, Connie snapped the map that she was holding. "It's straight up this highway, Bea. No twists, no turns. For goodness sakes, we can't get lost!"

"Humph!" Hattie's less than subtle insinuation needed no further explanation, but of course she had to add, "Bea, the speed limit is 65." The speedometer read 67 m.p.h., which was much too fast as far as she was concerned.

This was the first road trip by car that the three women had taken together. Their usual mode of transportation was by bus with the Road Wanderers, a group of fellow retirees. This was a new experience—a *very* interesting one.

"I've got to pee," Connie informed them. "And I'm hungry too." Her stomach growled on cue to confirm the declaration. "You've got to stop somewhere so that I can get something to eat." Connie wiggled in her seat uncomfortably. "If I don't get someplace soon I'm going to use it right here on the front seat."

"I've got you." The threat alone was enough to make Bea pull off the road at the next exit. Two sharp rights later they sat parked in front of a tiny variety store cluttered with advertising in its dirt streaked windows. Parked next to them was a bright red jalopy sporting a yellow streak of lightning across its side. Its occupants, two young leather-clad men with blue and green hair respectively, and pierced ears, noses and lips, peered at the three women suspiciously. The ladies returned their stares.

"I changed my mind. I don't have to pee that bad,"

Connie whispered to Bea out of the corner of her mouth. "Let's get the hell out of here!"

Bea didn't have to be asked twice. She wasted no time getting back on the highway. The three women breathed a collective sigh of relief.

"What in the world was that?" Bea looked in the rear-view mirror to see if they were being followed.

"Young people expressing themselves, I guess." Connie continued to wiggle in her seat.

"You let me find one of my grandkids coming to me with blue or green hair, and you'll see how I'll express *myself*." Hattie settled back in her seat feeling a bit more secure now that they had put distance between them and the last exit. "Of course, you wouldn't find my grandbabies running around here looking like that . . . "

Bea and Connie gave each other *the look*, their silent message to each other to tune out the rest of the conversation. Hattie was about to talk about her grandchildren—again. There were four of them, two by each of her two children. According to their doting grandmother, they were all perfect. Any topic would bring up the subject of her grandkids. If she brought out their pictures, the listener was in for a marathon conversation. Taking the initiative, Bea interrupted Hattie's latest discourse.

"There's a restaurant. I'm pulling off at this exit."

She pulled off the highway into the parking lot of a fast food restaurant. Leaping from the car, Connie raced across the lot and into the building anxious to get to the ladies room. Bea and Hattie were just ordering breakfast when Connie rejoined them. When their orders were filled, the three of them found a table.

"How much further do we have to go?" Hattie

inquired, stretching the kinks from her body. "I'm stiff as a board already."

"We've only been on the road an hour." Connie dug into her plate of pancakes like a starving refugee. "And if you would exercise instead of sitting around complaining about everything, you wouldn't be so stiff."

Hattie bristled, prepared to deliver a sharp retort. Bea intervened.

"I still can't believe that he's gone."

"Well he is," Hattie said bluntly. "Dead as a doornail." Hattie took a sip of coffee, oblivious to Bea's pained expression.

Connie's fork stopped in midair. "You're so sensitive, Hattie." She cut her eyes at her.

"What? What did I say? He *is* dead."

"You never liked him anyway." Bea's tone was venomous. She still remembered how her best friend had criticized her decades ago when she ended her engagement to Frank. She had said that Frank was weak, and that it was her fault that he had been vulnerable to the charms of another woman.

"That's not true!" Hattie's surprise was genuine. "I always liked Frank. It was his choice for a wife that I didn't like."

"Well like her or not, from what I hear, Charlie Mae, *Charmain* or whatever the hell she calls herself is going to be a very rich widow." Connie's interest was in the practical side of the situation.

"No doubt. Frank was a wealthy man." Bea pushed her plate of eggs and sausage aside. It had barely been touched, and her coffee cup remained full. Since hearing about Frank's death, food had lost its appeal. "Now, that woman is going to get everything he worked so hard for, and all because their divorce wasn't final."

"*Divorce!*" Hattie and Connie reacted simultaneously. The looks of shock, surprise and betrayal were written clearly on their faces.

"Oh, I thought I told you," Bea responded sheepishly. "Frank and Charlie Mae were getting a divorce."

Hattie was stone-faced. "No, you didn't tell us."

"I don't believe this!" Connie chided. "That's all you've done for the last three weeks is talk about that man. How could you have left something that important out?"

"I'm sure that there was a lot she left out," Hattie cracked. The pending divorce heightened her suspicions.

"So were Frank and you planning to get together before or after he dumped Charlie Mae?" Connie moved to the edge of her seat anxious for details.

Bea glowered at her friends, but Hattie wasn't intimidated. She was on a spiritual mission.

"No wonder you've been taking that man's death so hard. You and him planned on going to hell in a hand basket." She slammed her styrofoam cup on the table to emphasize her displeasure. "Now you know that you were wrong, Bea . . . "

"Don't start, Hattie, I really don't feel like hearing it. All I know is that Frank is dead, and the last time I saw him he looked like the picture of health. It's been days, and I still haven't been able to get information about how he died."

"I heard it was a stroke," Hattie offered.

"I told you that Thelma said that she heard that it was an aneurysm."

"And that's the problem! Nobody really knows what happened. It's all hearsay. I've called and called his office, and there's no answer. I guess they shut down after he died. I don't know. I called Houston, but all I get is his answering service. I don't know what to think." Her voice lowered to a tortured whisper. "Maybe it was this divorce thing putting too much stress on him." She closed her eyes fighting back the tears that threatened to flow.

Frank's death hit her harder than she had expected. She had tried to tell herself that the telephone calls that she and Frank had exchanged since the reunion and their subsequent dinner together were simply an exchange of greetings between old friends. Yet, she knew better. Each call offered an opportunity to mend past mistakes and brought hope for a future together, but with his death all hope was gone. It was that reality that lay heavy on Bea's heart. It made it difficult to accept that what they once had between them would never be again.

Clearing her throat, she pulled herself together. "All I know is that I want to be there to say one final goodbye." A lump caught in her throat. *This is only goodnight, not goodbye.* His words still haunted her. "And I want to know how he died. No, I *need* to know how he died. I want to know that whatever happened, he didn't suffer."

Her friends empathized. They knew how important this was to her. The death of Bea's son, James, Jr., had nearly destroyed her. She adored her two boys. What made the death of her child worse was that it had been slow and agonizing. He died from a rare form of bone cancer and had suffered greatly. He found peace only in death. The trauma of that experience was one that seemed to have effected every action that Bea took. Since then she had lived her life as if each day might be her last, no longer restrained by fear of the unknown.

Connie reached across the table and placed her hand

on top of her friend's folded hands. "Don't worry, Bea. We're only one hour from finding out the answer."

Hattie placed her hand on top of Connie's. "And I'm sure that Frank is looking down from heaven waiting for you to say that last goodbye."

Bea gave them a weak smile. That's what she liked about her girls, no matter how big the challenge or the disagreements they always ended up sticking together.

An hour later she wasn't too sure about that. They had arrived in Fort Wayne, and they were lost. The service was to begin at twelve noon, and that was fast approaching. The accusations were flying hot and heavy.

"You made the wrong turn when we exited, Bea!" Connie accused.

"You said, left! I turned left," Bea countered.

"I said right not left! Right!"

"It's your fault, Connie." Hattie jumped into the fray. "You didn't read the map right!"

"Both of you can shut up," Bea warned. "Or I swear I'll turn this car into a brick wall on purpose just to shut you up!"

"Lord, have mercy! I know you done lost your last mind, now. Give me that map, Connie. I can read it better than you."

"Sit back and be quiet, Hattie. You can't drive, so I know you can't read a map."

"Everybody sit back and be quiet!" Bea demanded. She pulled into a gas station determined to get her bearings and find the church. The two women complied but continued to throw each other malicious glares.

The petty sniping between Hattie and Connie had been going on so long that the three women had forgotten how it started and why. There was no doubt on either of their parts that they liked each other. If there had ever been doubt it ended the day Hattie's husband died. She had fallen completely apart, and like Bea, Connie had been there for Hattie and her family in every possible way. The favor had been returned when Connie's husband had died. So, despite the bickering the friendship between the three women was as solid as a rock.

Unbuckling her seatbelt, Bea started to get out of the car. Connie stayed her with a hand.

"Where are you going?"

"To find out where we are and to get directions." Bea got out and shut the door behind her. Time was running out. She didn't want to be late for the funeral. Charlie Mae probably wouldn't be welcoming anyway, so all she needed to do was to prance in late. Besides, Frank deserved the respect of her being there on time. He had always been a punctual man. Bea drew a shaky breath at the thought of Frank as she headed inside the gas station and convenience store.

A short while later the ladies were on their way with new directions tucked securely in Hattie's hands this time, at her insistence. Fifteen minutes later they pulled up in front of a huge red brick structure that looked more like a plantation big house than a Baptist church.

"This must be Charlie Mae's church," Hattie observed trying hard not to be impressed by the opulent edifice. "The Frank I knew wouldn't be caught dead in a place like this."

Connie rolled her eyes at the comment, unaware that Hattie was oblivious to its irony. Bea ignored them both as she sat gripping the steering wheel and staring up at the church. Frank was inside. This would be the last opportunity she would have to see him, the last place she wanted

to see him—dead and in a casket. She wasn't looking forward to the prospect. Yet, she was here. She *had* to be here.
She had to say that last goodbye.

After finding a parking spot, they had only minutes
to spare as they followed a group of other stragglers into
the church. The place was packed. It was a three-story
building, and the first two floors were filled to capacity.
They were directed to the third floor. A set of elevators
was available for the elderly and the disabled, but since
they thought of themselves as neither they climbed up the
three flights. Even when they arrived at the third tier they
still had to sit in the back row. It seemed that Frank Schaffer
was an important man in the city, and everyone who was
anyone in town was in attendance at his funeral.

After settling comfortably in the thick cushioned seats,
the three women examined their surroundings. The church
was magnificent. Decorated in white and gold, the ceiling
seemed to rise to eternity. Stained glassed windows, worth
a small fortune, adorned every window from floor to ceiling, admitting prisms of multicolored light that danced
like playful nymphs on snow white walls. The choir was
stationed in two suspended balconies on either side of the
pulpit. Dressed in gold and white they stood at rapt attention, with hymnals in hand as if ready to enter the pearly
gates any second. There was no doubt that this church was
the domain of the rich and powerful. Mink and sable clad,
six-figured income, Mercedes and BMW owners only were
allowed. All other sinners need not apply. The choir signaled the beginning of the service with a song—an anthem.

The eyes of all three women turned to the front of
the church. This was the moment Bea had dreaded. This
was the beginning of the goodbye. Her eyes scanned the
pulpit at the multitude of ministers. The program had

stated that even the mayor was there to say a few words. Opulent bouquets of flower were everywhere, spilling out onto the side aisles and surrounding two large pictures of the handsome man that Bea had once adored. Their fragrant aroma even reached the third tier.

"Where's Charlie Mae?" asked Connie, not pleased at all with their less than stellar seating arrangement, but aware that this was the price that latecomers paid.

No sooner had the words left her mouth did Charlie Mae appear, leaning heavily on the arm of a male escorting her down the aisle. Her stylish gray suit was trimmed in dyed gray mink as was the matching wide brimmed hat that she wore. Her sobs could be heard loud and clear throughout the church. Stopping, she swayed a little and uttered a poignant wail before being helped into her seat.

"Oh, brother!" Hattie muttered aloud, unconvinced by her performance. She returned the hostile stares of the more sympathetic mourners around her.

"Where's Frank?" Connie asked, straining to see the empty aisle Charlie Mae had just walked down.

"I don't know?" Bea had wondered about the absence of a coffin among the flowers. She hadn't really wanted to see him in that final state, but it would be her last chance to do so. "They must be wheeling his coffin in last." A moment of panic seized her at the thought that the casket might be closed. Surely Charlie Mae wouldn't do that.

"There's Houston." Hattie nodded her head toward Frank's younger brother as he slid onto the bench beside Charlie Mae.

"Yes, but where's Frank?" Bea repeated Connie's original question. The choir stopped singing and took their seats while a robe-clad minister stood and took his place behind the lectern. Bea frowned. Where *was* Frank? How could there be a funeral without a body? What was happening? Her eyes scoured the first floor anxiously.

"Brothers and Sisters we are here today to say goodbye to a great man." He made a sweeping gesture that stopped at the table placed beneath the lectern. It sat in the center of the array of flowers, between the two pictures sitting on gold plated easels.

"We've come to honor his memory and praise his time with us on earth."

"Yeah," Hattie whispered to Bea. "But where is *he*?"

"Brother Frank Schaffer is no longer with us, but his spirit will surely live on."

The minister's gesture was deliberate now and pointing straight to the table covered in gold lame. It contained a shiny brass vase covered with an ornate top. Bea hadn't noticed the item previously. Slowly it dawned on her that this was no flower vase as she had suspected earlier. This was—"No!" She gasped, drawing the attention of her friends.

"What's wrong?" Connie's forehead wrinkled with concern at the stricken look on Bea's face.

"You okay?" Hattie gripped Bea's arm. She didn't look good.

"That's Frank!" Bea's voice was a ragged whisper. She was unable to believe what she was seeing.

"Where?" Hattie came out of her seat as she strained to see Frank's casket being rolled down the aisle into the church.

"Not there. *There*!" Bea could hardly speak as she gestured toward the table. Their conversation was beginning to draw the attention of fellow mourners who seemed less than pleased with the talkative trio.

"Where?" It was Connie's turn to raise out of her seat.

"On the table!" Bea felt sick. This couldn't be true.

"Charlie Mae done put his body behind the table?" Hattie was incredulous. She knew the woman was tacky, but this was ridiculous!

"No! On the table! In the vase. I mean the urn."

She had to get out of here. This was too much! Standing, she pushed past Hattie and the other mourners as she made her way to the aisle, followed by her friends.

How she made it down the three flights of stairs was a blur. She stumbled outside with Hattie and Connie behind her. Once in the fresh air, Bea slumped against the brick building where she allowed the tears to flow.

"What is it, Bea? What were you talking about?" Connie's voice was full of concern.

"I'm talking about Frank, that's what!" She sniffed, buoyed by the memory of the wonderful man she knew and angered by what had become of him. "Frank was in that urn on the table."

"Say what!" Hattie looked shocked, while Connie still seemed puzzled, but Bea had worked herself into a rage.

"That slimy Charlie Mae done fried Frank and put him in a vase!"

CHAPTER 6

It was late when the three ladies returned from Fort Wayne. Bea was so upset that Connie drove them back home. Hattie was dropped off first, and she was just getting comfortable when the telephone rang. It had been a long tiring day, and she didn't feel like talking to anyone. She let the answering machine pick up the call. When she heard Dorothy's voice she grabbed the receiver.

"How was the funeral?" Dorothy asked without preamble.

"Well, good evening, Dorothy. I'm fine, how are you?" Hattie asked sarcastically.

"Girl, it's late, and I don't have time to fool around. How was the funeral?"

Hattie sighed. "Lord knows I'm not one to spread gossip, but it was pitiful."

"Well don't stop there. What was pitiful about it?" Dorothy pressed the receiver closer to her ear so that she wouldn't miss a word.

"First of all, there was no body!"

"You mean nobody was at the funeral?"

"No! Frank's body wasn't there—she burnt him up."

"Who did?"

"Charlie Mae! She cremated poor Frank and stuffed his ashes in a…ah…ah…what do they call that thing?"

"A jar?"

"No, that's not it."

"I know, a vase."

"No. A uni…ural."

"She put him in a urinal?"

"No!" Hattie thought for a minute. "An urn. That's it, she put him in an urn."

Dorothy was silent as she digested this information. "Let me get this straight. That woman actually cremated Frank, and there was no body?"

"That ain't the half of it," Hattie continued. "That hussy shed some crocodile tears, but Houston was all tore up. You know how close he was to Frank."

"Poor man, that *was* pitiful."

"The choir sang some off key song that nobody ever heard of. We all shed a tear about that. But the flower arrangements were beautiful. There were just tons of them, which shows how highly respected Frank was."

"Well, I figured he would have lots of flowers. I know it was crowded wasn't it?"

"Lord, yes. The people were spilling out of the church. Listen, we can talk about this later? I'm so tired, I've got to go to bed."

"Goodnight, Hattie. I'm going to turn in, too." Dorothy disconnected the call. She waited a second and quickly dialed Thelma's number.

"Girl, it's Dorothy, I know it's late, but guess what I just heard about Frank's funeral."

Thelma who had just settled in bed for the night sat up fully alert. "Let's hear it."

"You know Charlie Mae was always cold-blooded."

"Ain't it the truth! You remember when she tried to steal Leon from Hattie?"

" Whose boyfriend didn't she try to steal?" Dorothy grunted. "She always thought she was cute. You'll never guess what she did to poor Frank."

"What could she do? He's dead."

"Don't get smart. She went and cremated him."

"You're lying!"

"If I'm lying, I'm crying. She burned him up and put him in a solid gold urn."

"Gold? The show off."

"She must have sent invitations to the funeral. There were so many people, they had to pipe the services outside so everybody could hear."

"Say what?" Thelma could hardly believe it. "Why do you think she did that?"

"I heard it was a last minute decision to make way for the flowers because they had so many. You know a little urn don't take up much space."

"Did she take it hard?" Thelma asked eagerly.

"You know Charlie Mae. She's got to put on a show. She blubbered from one end of the church to the other. She grabbed the urn, hugging it like she'd never let go. Houston had to pry his dead brother from her hands."

"You mean what was left of him." Thelma paused thoughtfully. "I know it's late, and you probably want to get some sleep, so I'll talk to you later."

Thelma disconnected. She waited a second and quickly dialed Viola's number.

"It's me. Do you know what I just heard about Frank Shaffer's funeral?" She didn't wait for a response. "Who do you think had her husband cremated and put in a platinum urn placed on an ivory pedestal?"

"Wha-a-at? Tell me you're not talking about Charlie Mae? And a platinum urn? Leave it to her to show off."

"You know she thinks her shit don't stink. Now tell me how many black people do you know that cremate their loved ones?" Thelma was outraged.

Viola pondered the question. "Maybe they do that kind of thing where she comes from. You know Charlie Mae ain't from Indianapolis. She didn't move here from Fort Wayne until she was a junior in high school."

"Child, don't blame that on Fort Wayne!" Thelma retorted. "That's just some of Charlie Mae's craziness. But let me tell you the rest of it. She got to carrying on so at the funeral that she started hopping around the church and spilled the ashes."

"No!" Viola grabbed her telephone book thumbing through it frantically. "Girl, I've got to go. I'll talk to you later." She disconnected, found the number that she was looking for and quickly dialed it.

"Palmer residence," Connie answered sleepily.

"This is Viola, honey. I hate to wake you, but I heard about Frank's funeral. What's this about his ashes?"

"His ashes?"

"What happened at the funeral?" Viola asked impatiently. "What happened to his ashes?"

"From what I understand, Charlie Mae was going to bury them in a vault at the cemetery here in Indianapolis. I believe it was a private affair with just her and Houston." Connie was fully awake by now.

"How could Houston let her cremate his brother? Wasn't he upset?"

"I know he was upset about Frank's death, but I don't know how he felt about the cremation. He just looked upset in general. The poor man was crying so hard that he accidentally knocked over a plant as he was coming down the aisle to get in the pew. An usher swept up the dirt. It was a mess." Connie yawned.

"I won't keep you," Viola said, anxious to hang up. "You go back to sleep." Viola disconnected. She wasted no time calling Thelma. The phone was answered on the third ring.

"Are you awake?" Viola pressed on, not waiting for an answer. "Let me tell you what really happened at Frank's funeral because you got it all wrong. Houston *was* upset about his brother being cremated. He tried to hide it, but he just couldn't hold it in and took a swing at Charlie Mae."

"Shut up! Are you sure?"

"I got the story just now from Connie. She was there, so she ought to know. Anyway, when Charlie Mae ducked to avoid his fist he accidentally hit the urn instead. The usher had to vacuum up the ashes and put them in a can."

"Why didn't they put them back in the urn?"

"Cause the urn broke when it hit the floor! We just said Charlie Mae was all show. It wasn't platinum it was plastic!"

"Well why . . . "

"Stop interrupting." Viola was on a roll. "They had to seal the can before they put it in the vault."

"Didn't they bury the urn?"

"No, they don't bury urns. They put them in a vault."

"That's news to me. But let me call Dorothy and get this thing straight before it gets too late. The next thing you know all kinds of false rumors will get out."

It took several rings before Dorothy answered in a sleep-laden voice. "Hello. This had better be good."

Thelma was excited, "Girl, this *is* good. Why didn't you tell me the juicy stuff about Frank's funeral."

"I told you everything I heard."

"You didn't tell me about the fight."

"What fight?" Now Dorothy was excited.

"Houston took a swing at Charlie Mae during the service, and the ushers had to pull him off her. He knocked over some of the flowers *and* the urn. Since they couldn't separate the dirt from the ashes they vacuumed it all up and put it in a can."

Dorothy sat in stunned silence. "Tell me you're lying! I knew I should have gone to that funeral. What did they do with the can?"

"I think there was some sort of mix up about what they could do. You know, legally. So Charlie Mae put him in a bank vault until she can decide what to do," Thelma finished with a flourish and waited to see what impact her news would have.

"This is too much. I'm going to have to think about this and talk to you tomorrow. I've got to call Hattie and find out why she didn't tell me all this."

Dorothy disconnected and called Hattie. She didn't wait for a greeting.

"Hattie Collier! Why didn't you tell me about the fight?"

"Who is this? Dorothy? Do you know it's one thirty in the morning? What are you talking about?"

"You know what I'm talking about. The fight between Houston and Charlie Mae."

"You mean they had a fight? When?"

"At the funeral, girl. It was scandalous the way they were slugging it out at the service."

"Sweet Jesus! I knew we should have stayed through the whole thing." Hattie sighed in disgust. "I finally attend a funeral worth going to, and what happens? I miss all the good stuff."

CHAPTER 7

Hattie moved the cart down the aisle at a steady pace with Miss Fanny dragging along behind her. Lord knows she was trying to be patient with her mother-in-law, but the woman was complaining with every step she took. Hattie hated being at the woman's mercy, *literally*. Miss Fanny was eighty-something and still drove a car, no matter how slowly. Since their living arrangement became active, the two of them had managed to get where they were going, eventually, and that had been a plus for Hattie. It also made her think. If Miss Fanny could drive a car, as old and as mean spirited as she was, then there was nothing stopping her from learning to do so. Meanwhile, the only driving the woman was doing now was driving her crazy!

"You know that you're taking too long in here, don't you?" Miss Fanny whined. "Ain't that much shopping in the world. My feet are tired, and I'm ready to go."

"*Then go!*" Hattie wanted to shout, but instead she responded, "Why don't you go on out to the car, Miss Fanny. I'll go and see if they have those stockings I need, then meet you outside."

After briefly considering the suggestion, Miss Fanny agreed. Hattie watched her turn and shuffle down the aisle, relieved to have her out of her hair, at least temporarily. Happily she continued shopping.

Outside, the tired gait and slow shuffle that Miss Fanny had exhibited so dramatically inside the store disappeared as she stepped onto the parking lot with the vigor of a woman years younger.

"That Hattie gets on my last nerves," she muttered as she walked between the parked cars looking for her ten year old sedan. "She's the slowest woman I ever saw in my life! Now where did I park that car?"

Stopping, Miss Fanny's eyes scanned the lot slowly. All of the cars looked alike. Hattie had her so rattled with her list of places to go and things to do that she had forgotten to write down the number of the aisle in which she had parked, a habit that she had found necessary as she grew older. Presently she was at the back of the lot, and she still had no clue where her car was located.

She knew that it would be prudent to go back inside and wait for Hattie, whose memory might be better than her own, but she didn't want to give her the satisfaction of coming to the rescue. It would just confirm what Hattie thought, that she was old and forgetful. So for the next few minutes she roamed the parking lot, unsuccessful in her attempt to find the car.

Miss Fanny was just about to concede defeat when she spotted a couple at the end of one of the rows of cars. Perhaps they could help her. That is, if they could stop kissing long enough to take a breath. The couple was engaged in such a passionate embrace that the only thing missing was the bedroom. Deciding that they were too old to be out there on the parking lot carrying on like a couple of rabbits, Miss Fanny cleared her throat loudly.

"Excuse me!"

The couple jumped at the unexpected interruption. They turned to find the old woman standing before them. Miss Fanny's eyes slid from the medium height, brown skinned man who looked at her curiously, to the attractive, light brown skinned woman who had all but leaped from the man's arms. It was obvious that she was not happy about being interrupted. She glared at Miss Fanny whose attention turned back to the man.

"Sorry to bother ya'll, but I can't find my car, and I was wondering if you could help me out?"

The woman lifted a professionally arched eyebrow. "As you can see we're busy here. So *no*, we can't help you." She turned her back to Miss Fanny and started talking to the man.

Miss Fanny was shocked. The ornery heifer didn't need to be so nasty! On top of that, she had the nerve to be uppity too!

Miss Fanny started to give both of them a piece of her mind, but the couple walked away. Neither of them looked back to acknowledge her as they got into two separate cars parked next to each other. The smart aleck hussy got into a gray Mercedes, while her closed-mouthed companion slid behind the wheel of an older model American car.

"Humph!" Miss Fanny sniffed, studying both sets of license plates carefully. She stepped aside as the cars pulled out of their respective parking places and drove away. She made certain that she graced the woman with her most hateful stare.

Rolling her eyes at them as hard as she could, Miss Fanny continued her search. Luckily she met with success mere seconds before Hattie joined her in the car. Fanny drove out of the parking lot glad to be headed for home.

They were approaching the city's downtown area

when Hattie's telephone rang. Thelma was on the other end. She was in the beauty parlor waiting for her turn.

"Hey, Hattie, where you at?"

"Hi, Thelma. I'm on Madison Avenue. Miss Fanny and me just left the south side. What's going on?"

"Honey, I just had to fill you in on the latest about you-know-who. Big Mouth Roberta got the lowdown, and she's passing it on."

"I don't want to hear it. Charlie Mae Schaffer has done enough damage moving her wide tail back here to Indianapolis. She's spending poor Frank's hard earned money on that broke down mansion on Meridian street..."

"She's renovating it, Hattie."

"I don't care what you call it, she's a show off, and I don't want to hear nothing else about her. Anyway, Thelma, you know good and well that the Lord don't like gossip."

Dismissing Hattie's pseudo self-righteousness, Thelma sniffed.

"Then I won't tell you how she's bought a Bentley and has been running around here with a chauffeur driving it. You wouldn't be interested."

"You got that right." Hattie would die before she would let Thelma know that she had peaked her interest.

"All right then, Roberta is calling me. I've got to go." They disconnected.

Hattie turned to Miss Fanny. "Charlie Mae Schaffer! That's all everybody in this town can talk about. The woman comes back here to show us all up, and instead of ignoring her butt, everybody acts like she's the queen of the universe!"

Concentrating on the road, Miss Fanny didn't acknowledge Hattie's tirade at first. Then at a stoplight she slapped her palm against her forehead.

" Well, I'll be doggone! That's who that woman was!"

Hattie gave her a disinterested glance. "What woman?"

"The wench in the parking lot who got smart with me."

"What are you talking about, Miss Fanny? Who got smart with you?"

The red light turned green, and once again Miss Fanny's concentration was on the road. That was until the next red light.

"It was the woman that you were talking about. The one you and Bea was talking about when we went to visit her church a couple of weeks ago."

Hattie looked at her mother-in-law in exasperation. She had resumed the conversation out of the blue. Hattie could hardly remember the original topic. Miss Fanny had a way of doing that, and it drove her nuts, but the older woman was persistent.

"That woman! That woman! You know, the one that . . . " The light turned green again.

Hattie held her tongue. She could feel her blood pressure rising, but she waited patiently until the next red light. Miss Fanny resumed speaking.

"That Charlie Mae woman. She was the smart mouth in the parking lot with that man."

Man? Hattie's eyes widened. She uttered a quick, silent prayer to the Lord to hold the stoplight for an extra minute or so.

"What man, Miss Fanny?" She held her voice steady.

"The one she was slobbering on in the parking lot. They were all over each other like dogs in heat."

The light turned green, and Hattie almost choked. She could hardly contain herself. On the way home, between red lights, she got more details about the romantic tryst between Charlie Mae and the mystery man. From the description Miss Fanny gave her, the woman was definitely Charlie Mae. She even described the car that she was driving—the same one that she had driven the Sunday that she came to visit Bea's church. Charlie Mae had hardly made herself discrete. She had made a major production of contributing a small fortune to the church's building fund.

By the time Hattie got home she nearly knocked the front door down in her effort to get to the telephone and call Bea and Connie.

Bea answered on the second ring. Hattie was breathless.

"*Girrrrl!* Do I have something to tell you. Dial Connie. We've *got* to have a three way on this one!"

CHAPTER 8

Connie and Bea were shopping with their granddaughter, Tina, for a dress for the junior prom, when it became clear that their outing was probably a mistake. Each of them had a different taste in fashion, and they couldn't agree on anything. After going through nearly every store at the upscale mall in which they were shopping, Connie suggested that they break for lunch. They had made reservations at one of the popular eateries in the mall where Hattie and Miss Fanny joined them. The waitress ushered them to their table.

"I thought we were going to be late," Hattie apologized, giving her mother-in-law a pointed look. Miss Fanny opened her mouth to defend herself, but Bea intervened in an effort to diffuse an argument.

"You're here now, so everything's all right."

The waitress took their orders. Everyone ordered a light lunch to leave room for their favorite desserts then sat back to enjoy one another's company.

"So, how did the shopping go?" Hattie asked Tina, bestowing a warm smile on the pretty young girl.

"Fine." Tina didn't sound too convincing. "If I don't mind being dressed like a twelve year old." It was clear that she wasn't happy with how the shopping excursion had gone so far.

"I liked the peach dress, but it just showed too much of your body," Bea explained.

"Okay, you two," Connie interjected, "we've fought over dresses for half the morning. Why don't we just give it a rest for today." Bea and Tina agreed.

After lunch the five of them strolled the mall casually window-shopping before heading outside to their cars. Hattie, Bea and Connie walked ahead of Tina and Miss Fanny, busily engaged in conversation that revolved around Charlie Mae and her mysterious lover.

"I've tried and tried, and I can't imagine who this man could be." Bea's brow furrowed as she pondered the issue.

Connie had a suggestion. "Have you considered everyone at your church?"

Bea rolled her eyes in frustration. Of all the churches in the city that woman had brought her substantial behind over to where *she* was a member. Since the Sunday that Charlie Mae joined the Church of the Living Unity of Christ's Kingdom Missionary Baptist church, or CLUCK Baptist as it was affectionately called, Bea had tried to figure out why.

"I don't think it's anyone from church. Surely she's not that stupid."

The three women were standing deep in thought considering that possibility when Miss Fanny and Tina caught up with them.

"Hattie?" Miss Fanny called, but there was no response. She tried again. "Hattie?"

"Miss Fanny, can you hold it for just a minute." She glanced at the woman absently. "We're trying to figure something out."

"But Hattie—"

Beleaguered, Hattie turned her eyes heavenward as she muttered a silent prayer. "Lord, please give me the strength to do my Christian duty by this woman cause you know she gets on my last nerve."

"Hattie?" Miss Fanny was persistent.

Turning to her mother-in-law, Hattie responded as sweetly as she could. "Now Miss Fanny, I know you're ready to go, but can't you just wait a few more minutes? We're trying to figure out who the man was you saw with Charlie Mae last week. It's called brainstorming, and it won't take long."

The older woman fumed. Her eyes were daggers. "Don't you dare talk down to me, Hattie Collier. I'm old, but I am not a fool. And if you stop acting so high and mighty, you might be interested to know that the man is standing right under your nose."

Everyone, including Tina, looked at Miss Fanny as though she had lost her mind. The old lady gestured with her head in the direction of the parking lot. Four pairs of eyes turned in that direction. A medium height, black man wearing a leather jacket was rapidly approaching them. He veered through a row of cars before he reached them. Excited, the women all began talking at once.

"You are talking about that man aren't you?"

"Is that the man you saw with Charlie Mae?"

"Why didn't you say something?"

Bea tried to calm everyone down. "Be quiet, everybody. Come on, Connie, he looks like he's headed toward the part of the lot where we're parked. Let's follow him."

She turned back to Miss Fanny. "Can you and Hattie take Tina home?"

"Grandmother, I want to come," Tina spoke up

quickly. She wasn't sure what was happening, but she wanted to get in on the action. "You guys will need all the eyes you can get." She paused thoughtfully. "And it's not like he knows we're following him. By the way, who are we following and why?"

With no time to argue or to explain, Bea and Connie rushed through the lot to their car with Tina close behind. Managing to keep up with the stranger at a discrete distance, they followed his car as it turned west onto 86th Street. Making sure that she wouldn't lose him, Bea lurched through the next light a millisecond after it turned red.

Connie grabbed the dashboard. "I should be driving. You know you can't keep up with this guy."

"Oh yeah? You just watch me." Bea swerved into the far right lane and squeezed between two cars with mere inches to spare.

Tina was grinning with excitement. "Grandmother, you've never driven this fast before. You go, Grandmother!"

"I'm trying to keep up." Bea's adrenaline was pumping. "But I don't know why he's driving so fast."

The car they were tailing turned onto the interstate. Bea was several car lengths behind.

"Now I *know* I should have driven," Connie moaned as the car temporarily disappeared from sight.

Bea made no comment as she leaned forward and pushed down on the gas pedal. She wore a look of determination on her face. The car reappeared, and Bea increased her speed.

Tina clapped her hands and began to chant, "Go Grandma! Go Grandma! Go!"

"Tina!" both grandmothers scolded.

They zipped down the highway at a speed close to 80

mph. Still the car they were following pulled away from them.

"Bea, can't you go any faster?" wailed Connie. "He's getting away!"

With her hand in a vice grip on the steering wheel, Bea attempted to catch sight of the car by switching lanes. Connie spotted the car.

"There he is!" Connie shrieked excitedly.

"But I can't see him," Bea complained.

"Grandma?" Tina addressed Connie.

"I knew I should have driven," Connie said, preoccupied with the chase.

"Grandmother." Tina addressed Bea this time. Since early childhood she had distinguished between the two by addressing Bea more formally. However, at the moment neither woman seemed to be acknowledging her. She tried again.

"Hey, you guys, the car behind us . . . "

"Will you look at this idiot tailgating me like that?" Bea glared in her rearview mirror, citing the car behind her. "I can't believe the way some people drive!"

"Grandmother, I think he wants you to pull over," Tina explained.

"And why should I do that?" Bea was indignant. "There are two other lanes on either side of me. He can just go around."

"I really think you need to pull over," Tina explained quietly. "It's a cop."

"A what!" Bea gawked into the rearview mirror with disbelief. The trooper signaled for her to pull over onto the shoulder of the highway. Bea did so. She swallowed nervously as he climbed out of his vehicle and approached her car.

"Do you ladies know how fast you were going?" The trooper peered through the open driver's window as he addressed the car's three occupants.

"Officer, I may have been going a little fast, but I was trailing a suspect who was going faster than me." Bea smiled up at him solicitously. "I didn't see you pull *him* over."

"Excuse me?" The officer looked surprised.

"It's a long story, but the man I was trailing is involved with the wife of an old friend. Actually, he's dead, but my girlfriend's mother-in-law saw them together, and I thought he could lead us to some kind of clue . . . "

"Clue? Clue to what?" The young officer looked as confused as she sounded. "May I see your license and registration, please?"

"Yes you may, but I want you to know I never speed, and if I wasn't on this case, I wouldn't be speeding now. Just ask my son, Bryant Bell. He's a policeman."

The two women watched the trooper walk back to his vehicle. When he was out of earshot, Connie asked nervously, "Do you think you should have given that much information to a police officer? And especially that lie about your being on some sort of case?"

"Relax, Connie. And we are on a case. What else would you call it?"

"I'm tempted to call it insanity," Connie retorted. "I know how you felt about Frank, but I'm not sure about all this following people."

Tina tapped the two women on their shoulders. "He's coming back."

"Looks like you're okay, ladies." The officer returned Bea's license and registration. He took off his sunglasses to emphasize his point. "I don't know what it is you think you're doing, but in the future I would advise you to slow down. I'm letting you off with a warning this time, but if you're caught speeding again, it will be an automatic ticket."

After dropping Tina off, Bea and Connie arrived at Hattie's house. Hattie took one look at their dejected faces and guessed that their novice attempt at car trailing had not been the success they had envisioned.

"It doesn't matter," Bea said, putting the best spin possible on the situation. "We could ask Bryant to trace the license plate. That is, if we had gotten the number."

"Don't tell me you didn't get it?" Hattie shook her head at their amateurish exploits.

"We just didn't think of it," Connie admitted. "Once we took off on the highway we never got close enough."

As the three friends argued over who should have gotten the license plate number and who should have driven, Miss Fanny walked into the room. She cleared her throat. The women continued to squabble. Miss Fanny cleared her throat again, louder this time. Her presence wasn't acknowledged.

"334!" she said as loudly as she could.

This time she caught Bea's attention. "What are you saying, Miss Fanny?"

"334 is what I said," the older woman repeated. There was defiance in her voice.

"What is that supposed to mean?" Hattie looked at her mother-in-law with raised eyebrows. Had she finally lost her mind?

"Don't look at me like that, Hattie. Do you think I'm some kind of idiot? I don't like being patronized? And I'll tell you what it means. It's the first three numbers of the license plate."

The three looked at her as though she had grown an extra head. How could she possibly know the license plate number of the car that they followed? She hadn't been part of the chase. Hattie walked over to her and took her gently by the arm.

"Now Miss Fanny, I know it's been a long day, and you're tired. I appreciate you trying to help, but we've got a serious matter here, and we need to figure out what to do next."

Miss Fanny shook herself loose from Hattie's grip. "Just like I said. You think I'm an idiot, but I've got news for you. When I saw those two in the parking lot, and they were so nasty to me, I knew I had seen that woman before. Since I couldn't remember where, I wrote down both their license plate numbers because they acted suspicious."

"Yes, I do remember you writing something down before we drove off," Hattie confirmed thoughtfully.

"Well, they could have been criminals or something," Miss Fanny said, taking a piece of paper from her pocket. She waved it in front of her.

Grinning, Hattie was so excited that she hugged the older woman. "That was good thinking. What is the rest of the number?"

"Oh no," declared Miss Fanny, "I'm just a doddering old lady. In fact, I might have put the wrong numbers down. You just go on and figure out a way to track that car down yourself."

Hattie tried to maintain her temper. How dare this old woman black mail her! "Okay, if you want an apology, then I apologize. Now *please* can we have the number?"

Miss Fanny looked down at the paper thoughtfully. "I don't know if you're really sincere so I'm going to sleep on it." She started off to her room but stopped and turned around. "If you want my help, there had better be some changes around here." She pocketed one slip of paper and produced another from a second pocket.

"What's that?" asked a curious Hattie.

With a sly smile Miss Fanny answered triumphantly, "Here is my list of demands."

CHAPTER 9

At nine o'clock the next morning Bea was in the police wing of the City County Building pleading her case. Her son Bryant was the younger of her two boys and a 10-year veteran of the department. She had to admit that he cut quite a figure in his police uniform. Her son was a good-looking man. He had a chestnut brown complexion with a long, angular intelligent looking face and dark brown eyes that he inherited from his late father. The expression on his face was usually serious, but now it was one of concern.

"Mom, this is not police business, and even if it were, it is not *your* business." He spoke in a hushed tone, being careful that none of his colleagues were within earshot.

"Bryant, of course it's police business. This could be the license plate number of a criminal." Bea emphasized her point by waving the piece of paper under his nose.

"You don't know what we had to go through to get this license plate number."

Taking the paper from his mother's hand he begged for some glimmer of understanding. "First of all, you don't know if this car belongs to a criminal. Second, if I found out that it did I wouldn't be happy knowing that you've been trying to chase him down, and third, I am not a detective investigating a case. I'm a patrolman." As soon as the last words were out of his mouth he was sorry.

"I know, Sweetie, and I've begged you over and over again to take the examination for detective. You have a brilliant mind, and you could be the best detective this place has seen."

"Mom." He gave her a stern look.

"All I want is to find out who owns this plate. After all, the man could be dangerous if he knows we're on to him and Charlie Mae."

"I would become dangerous too if I thought you were meddling in my love life. What's up with you and this Mrs. Schaffer? You've been complaining about her for months. You treat her like she committed a murder or something." Bryant looked around, conscience that his voice was raising with each exasperating question.

"I hadn't thought of that." Bea's voice trembled with excitement. "You might be right. We know she's an adulteress. She may very well be a murderer too. Her husband's death *was* rather sudden."

"I thought you said he died of a heart attack?"

"That's what I finally found out, but you're a policeman. Aren't means, motive and opportunity the three things that spell murder? It's all there. So please, son, all I want is the name of the owner of this car. What if this is something that could help earn you a promotion? Come on, do me this favor just this once, and I'll never bother you again."

Bryant's shoulders slumped in defeat. "Wait here. I'll be back in a few minutes."

Bea settled back contentedly. She had been confident her son would help. She could always count on him. Bryant returned shortly. She could tell by his stone-face expression that he was not happy with what he had found.

"Well," he said, "it didn't take long to find out who owned the plate. Now what I'd like to suggest that you do is go home and forget this whole thing."

"Why?" Bea was on instant alert. Her son only used that tone when he was upset. "What did you find out? It belongs to some criminal, doesn't it?"

"No, it belongs to Roosevelt Feathers."

Bea frowned. That name sounded vaguely familiar. She tried to remember where she'd heard it before. Then her mouth fell open in surprise.

"Isn't Roosevelt Feathers . . . "

"Yes, Mother, Roosevelt Feathers, is a former lieutenant in this police department. The man you were following is a retired cop."

* * * *

"Bryant said it could be a case of foul play," Bea recounted to Hattie, as she reported on her meeting with her son earlier that morning. "Something I hadn't thought about."

Hattie was skeptical. "Did he really say that?"

"Well, he implied it," Bea said defensively.

The two women stood in the sanctuary of CLUCK Baptist. The sound of the sanctuary doors opening drew their attention as Charlie Mae Schaffer entered and strutted down the aisle toward them. She was wrapped in a floor length silver fox mink.

Charlie Mae had made quite a splash since her move back to Indianapolis, first the purchase of a mansion on Meridian street, near the Governor's mansion, and then being squired around town in a chauffeur driven Bentley.

Yet that paled next to the impression that she had made when she joined CLUCK Baptist. Since becoming a member, the pastor and his flock had begun to treat Mrs. Frank Schaffer—as she preferred to be called—as though she were the Second Coming. Of course a generous donation to the church's building fund had helped fuel that devotion, to say nothing of the new choir robes she had purchased.

Neither Bea nor Hattie had any objection to a sinner trying to repent. That was the purpose of going to church. However, they did object to Charlie Mae's rush up the ranks of the anointed when she knew that she had a stain on her record named Roosevelt Feathers—a married man.

"You know good and well its too hot for her to be wearing that fur coat," Hattie muttered to Bea, not trying to conceal her contempt for the woman who was rapidly approaching. "My guess is that she's in practice for roasting in hell."

Bea couldn't hold the laughter as Charlie Mae, flanked by her two buddies, Rosemary Sanders and Laverne Nelson, stopped in front of them.

"Hello, ladies." Her smile reflected the sincerity of her greeting.

Bea nodded. "Charlie Mae." Hattie simply gave her a blank stare.

Sighing her displeasure at Bea's refusal to address her by her adopted name, Charlie Mae looked at her pointedly. "I guess you heard that everyone isn't pleased with the way that you've been running the fundraiser for the Missionary Society."

"No, I hadn't heard that," Bea retorted, trying to keep her surprise at the revelation out of her voice. "Not one person has come directly to me and voiced such an opinion, except *you*."

"Why don't you tell us about that, Charlie Mae?" Hattie added snidely.

Charlie Mae turned to her with a smug smile. "I wasn't aware that you were a member of this church, Hattie. I thought that you still belonged to that quaint little storefront that your father pastored. That is, when he wasn't cleaning toilets as a janitor."

Hattie didn't blink. "No, I'm not a member here, but I am a friend of Bea's, and any place that I can help with the Lord's work I do so, not that she really needs it. After all, you might not be familiar with the fact that her fundraising ideas have raised vast amounts of money for the Missionary Society each year. This one won't be any different, I'm sure."

"Oh, really?" Charlie Mae smirked. "We'll see."

Haughtily, she moved past the two women with her small entourage. After a brief knock on the door, they disappeared into the pastor's study.

"That woman's up to something." Bea stared at the closed door.

"No doubt about that," Hattie agreed. "And only the good Lord, or more likely Satan, knows what it is."

* * * *

Connie savored her morning cup of tea with relish. That's what she liked about semi-retirement. She could work when and if she wanted or simply spend time enjoying a good cup of tea and the morning paper. What a life!

Systematically, she thumbed through the pages of the daily newspaper. She always started with the real estate section, and then she went to the business section. Sometimes she reviewed the entertainment page if she was considering going to a movie or a play. Usually she ended her morning ritual with the front page. It was rare for her to read the obituary section. Unlike Hattie, she didn't scour the obituary for the funeral of strangers. The woman had actually planned every detail of her own funeral in advance, and occasionally did revisions when she found something new to add that she liked. Thank God, most of the people that Connie knew were too busy living their lives to occupy themselves with death and dying. So when she scanned the obituaries and her eye landed on the name of a woman named Cheryl, she started to turn the page. She didn't know anyone named Cheryl, but the name Feathers—now where had she heard that name before?

The answer hit her like a lightening bolt. Carefully, she read the short article accompanying the woman's picture. It contained the information that she was 48 years old and had died in a boating accident two days ago. She had left three survivors: Her mother, Mrs. Easter Gaddis. No, Connie didn't know her. Her sister, Mrs. Sandy Cruise. That name wasn't familiar either. Then there was her husband, former police lieutenant Roosevelt Feathers. Connie sat up and took notice. *Bingo!*

CHAPTER 10

Bea and Hattie were in a meeting room in the basement of CLUCK Baptist reviewing plans for the church fundraiser when Charlie Mae approached the closed door. They were so engrossed in conversation that they didn't notice her through the glass window that looked into the room. Charlie Mae opened the door without knocking and stood in the entranceway observing them. Her two cohorts were no longer with her.

"Well, well, well, what do we have here? A little strategy session?"

Momentarily startled by the unexpected intrusion, Bea met her taunting gaze. "And what would we be having a strategy session about?" Bea paused before deliberately adding, "*Charlie Mae?*" She watched in silent delight as the woman visibly bristled.

"Perhaps you and your shadow there need to work overtime to come up with a way to prevent me from raising more money than you this year for the Missionary Board."

"Who are you calling a shadow?" Hattie started to rise in challenge, but Bea held her in place.

"Why don't you simply donate the money, Charlie Mae?" asked Bea. "You seem to buy everything else that you want."

"Except a place in heaven," Hattie snarled, still smarting from her previous remark.

Charlie Mae ignored her as she addressed Bea. "I don't want to buy this one. This time the pleasure will be in the victory."

"I see. Well, I guess if that's the only way you can get your pleasure out of life, there's hardly anything I can do about it is there?"

Charlie Mae's smile was lethal. "No, you're right, Bea. There's absolutely *nothing* that you can do about me." With the confidence of a dowager queen, she pulled her fur coat tighter around her and swept down the hallway.

"That two-by-four heifer," spat Hattie, forgetting momentarily that she was a Christian. "I've been wanting to kick her behind since high school. I ought to catch up with her and do just that!"

"And what would be the point?" Bea sighed in resignation. "You two would look like fools fighting like teenagers, and in church too."

Hattie conceded, "You're right, I don't want to be on record for perpetrating violence in the House of the Lord. But I'm telling you that woman got the devil in her, and he's had a hold of her a long time—cheating on poor Frank. We should have called her out on it. That would have given her something to think about."

"She probably would have denied it."

"I know it, but we could have shaken her up a little. She's been a snob since we were kids. Don't you remember when her fast butt first came to Attucks? She thought she was hot stuff."

"At the time I thought that was because she felt insecure being the new girl in school."

" Insecure my behind! Charlie Mae thought she was better than us. She thought that light skin, long hair and a big butt gave her privileges."

"It did then." Bea tossed her papers into the binder she was carrying as she prepared to leave. "And don't pretend that it didn't. Come on, let's go."

Hattie packed up as well. "Yeah, you're right, but she was extra nasty with flaunting her stuff. It wasn't like her family was well off or nothing." She was still smarting from Charlie Mae's earlier remark about her father. "They were struggling like the rest of us black folks. Shoot, her family was boarding with some other family when they first moved here from Ft. Wayne."

"With her uncle, if I remember correctly." Bea moved out of the meeting room and down the hallway with Hattie following.

"Uh, uh, she lived in the ghetto just like the rest of us. She was always talking about how much she hated Indianapolis and how Ft. Wayne was so much nicer, as if anybody cared."

Bea chuckled. "Let it go, Hattie. That was so long ago it's a forgotten memory." The two women stepped out of the church's side door into the parking lot.

"Oh, like you've let go of the past, huh?" Hattie sniffed. "I ain't the one running around here mourning over an old boyfriend from high school who just happened to be somebody *else's* husband." She raised a challenging brow.

Bea cut her eyes at her friend as they sauntered across the parking lot to her car. "I'm just concerned that Frank's wishes were so blatantly ignored. I know for sure that he didn't want to be cremated when he died. He told me so. It just disturbs me to no end that she would do something like that."

"Maybe she was trying to destroy evidence," Hattie quipped. "That's how them black widow spiders do it on . . . Lord have mercy!"

Hattie screamed and leaped back in horror as a delivery truck barreled into the parking lot narrowly missing her. The truck came to a screeching stop near the church. A uniformed employee jumped from the vehicle and hurried over to Hattie. His face was red with embarrassment.

"I'm so sorry! Are you all right?" The young man's distress was obvious. "I didn't see you!"

"I guess you didn't, speeding around here like a bat out of hell!" Hattie wasn't in a forgiving mood.

"You're right." The man's blue eyes darted from Hattie to Bea nervously, seeking an ally. "I was just trying to make time." Bea looked at him unsympathetically. His eyes slid back to Hattie. "I'm really sorry."

Grumbling, Hattie swiped imaginary dirt from her dress. "Well, you better watch what you're doing next time, and stop driving like a wild man. You better be glad I'm not hurt. I could have broken a couple of bones, or worse."

"You're right, ma'am, and again I'm sorry." With the hope that he had avoided a call of complaint to his supervisor he started backing away toward the truck. "It won't happen again, believe me." He turned and trotted back to his truck.

"You didn't hurt anything did you?" asked Bea, examining her friend from head to foot. Hattie shook her head in the negative as she started to get into the car, but curiosity stopped her as she watched the driver exit from the truck with an arm filled with boxes.

"Hey, young man!" she shouted, drawing his attention. "What have you got there?"

Stopping, he glanced down at the boxes in his arms. "It's something from a publishing house." He read the name aloud. It was unfamiliar to all three of them. He looked on the side of the box. "It says here that the boxes contain bibles." He rounded the truck and knocked on the side door of the church.

"You can go on in," Bea directed from inside the car through an opened window. She then addressed Hattie. "Come on, we've got to go."

Hattie stood rooted with the car door open looking indecisive as her eyes followed the delivery man's movements. She turned to Bea.

"You didn't say anything about your church getting new bibles." A touch of envy was in her tone. CLUCK Baptist was always receiving blessings, while small churches like her own continued to struggle.

"It's not an everyday topic of conversation, Hattie," Bea said impatiently. "Now get in. I have to pick Tina up."

Hattie turned her attention back to the now unoccupied delivery truck. "Ain't you curious about those bibles? What they look like?"

Bea sighed her increasing annoyance. "No! I've got to go! Now get in before I leave you!"

The delivery man exited the church door and went back inside the truck to gather additional boxes. He was followed by one of the deacons who came out to help. Fortunately, it was a deacon that Hattie knew. Much to Bea's chagrin, she scurried over to where the two men were unloading the remaining boxes.

"Oh, Brother Jacobs! Brother Jacobs!"

He greeted Hattie with a familiar smile. "Hello, Sister Collier. What can I do for you?"

"Oh, I was just wondering if I could get a look at those new bibles ya'll unloading. We've been discussing replacing our old worn out bibles over at my church, and I wanted to see the ones ya'll got." Hattie ignored Bea's loud blast on the horn as she stood looking at Brother Jacobs expectantly. He had been a member of her father's church when they were younger, but for the last decade he had been a member of CLUCK Baptist. Hattie still considered him a defector, and her stance told him that he had no choice but to grant her request. Brother Jacobs complied.

Resting the boxes he was holding on the stone wall that bordered the walkway, he withdrew a small penknife attached to his key ring. He slit the tape binding the top box, opened it and withdrew the stuffing and then a bible. Another blast of Bea's horn interrupted the morning quiet.

"Sounds like Sister Bell is ready to go." He nodded toward the car in which a sour faced Bea sat fuming.

"Oh, she'll be all right." Eagerly, Hattie reached for the bible in his hand. It was bound in white leather, with the words Holy Bible written on the cover in gold. The edges of the pages were gold leaf.

"It's beautiful," Hattie breathed in awe. "Let me show Bea."

She hurried across the church parking lot and slid into the front seat of the car, ignoring the glower Bea gave her.

"I'm getting ready to leave you, and I mean it!"

Hattie shoved the bible into her hand. "Look at this, Bea. Isn't it the most beautiful bible you've seen?"

Bea started to fuss about her inconsiderate behavior, but was caught off guard as the grainy leather was slipped into her hand. The book *was* beautiful. She ran her fingers over the raised gold lettering. It was also expensive.

"I didn't know that we could afford something like this." Her brows knitted in puzzlement. She had just opened the book when her cell phone rang. She scrambled to answer it. "Bea speaking." Connie was on the other end. Bea listened intently to what was being said.

"What page is it on?" she asked. Her voice registered keen interest.

"What page is *what* on?" Hattie echoed.

Bea held up a silencing finger as she listened to Connie, then: "I'm going to buy a newspaper on my way home. I can't wait to read this!"

Disconnecting, Bea turned to Hattie and shared the news that Connie had just delivered. Hattie turned it over in her head.

"So now that his wife is dead, you're saying that Roosevelt Feathers is free, and so is Charlie Mae?" Hattie wanted to get her facts straight.

Bea pondered Hattie's comment. "That's quite a coincidence, huh?" She started to close the bible she was holding, when the dedication on the front page caught her attention. It read:

This holiest of books is being donated to the Church of the Living Unity of Christ Kingdom Missionary Baptist Church by Mrs. Charmaine Schaffer in memory of her beloved husband, Frank Schaffer. You have my love and my loyalty always.

"Love and loyalty!" Bea slammed the book shut. The look on her face was visceral. "That's the final straw! If it's the last thing I do on earth, I'm bringing Charlie Mae Crenshaw down!"

CHAPTER 11

"The former police lieutenant explained that his wife was a good swimmer, but that she hadn't been swimming in years and may have panicked. 'All we wanted was a little romantic outing on the reservoir,' said the distraught husband." Bea looked up from the newspaper article she was reading and grunted a dubious "Ha!" before continuing. "And I ended up losing the love of my life."

"Oh, please!" Hattie rolled her eyes.

"You need a pair of boots to wallow in that shit," said Connie.

Hattie shot her a warning look. "You know I don't like that cussing."

Bea folded the copy of the newspaper article she had just read and placed it in her purse. It was only one of a number of copies she had retrieved from her trek to the public library yesterday. She had been compelled to do so as the result of the telephone call to her from Connie, providing her with the information about Roosevelt Feather's wife. Something smelled fishy about this whole thing. First, Charlie Mae's declarations of undying love for Frank, in spite of the fact that they were divorcing and that she had a lover, was suspect. Now there was the death of her lover's wife. Both served to heighten Bea's suspicions. She had gone straight to the library right after she dropped Hattie off.

Searching back issues of the city's newspapers to find out more about the death of Cheryl Feathers, she discovered a lot about the couple as well. It seemed that the Feathers had been quite the socialites, although she never had run into them at any of the functions she attended. After all, she did get around quite a bit herself. The couple had graced the social pages of several local publications over the years.

The story of the drowning had been a short one buried in the back pages of the newspaper a few days ago. According to the article, the boat had overturned on Eagle Creek Reservoir. Roosevelt had swum safely to shore, but Cheryl Feathers had drowned.

It was simply luck that Connie had stumbled across the obituary. However, it was by design that the ladies were here at the mortuary. Bea had recruited her two friends to help her launch an investigation into what she considered to be foul play. Only Connie had brought up the question of what they could possibly be investigating.

"Now tell me again what we're looking for in here and why we're doing this?"

"I'm gong to be honest with you, Connie," Bea said, unsure about the answer to that question. "The whole thing just looks a little suspicious to me. Frank dies suddenly . . . "

"Of a heart attack," the practical Connie reminded her.

"I know, but he dies in the process of divorcing a cheating wife who ends up with a fortune!"

"But did he know that she was cheating?" Connie

asked, still not convinced that Bea's reasoning was sound. "Did he tell you that was the reason for the divorce?"

"No, he didn't, and I don't know if he knew or not," Bea answered honestly, "but I know that he didn't want to be cremated. That came straight from his mouth. Surely he said the same thing to his own wife."

"So why did she cremate him?" Hattie asked.

"It could have been spite," Connie offered, less excited than Hattie about today's activity.

"Or she could have done it to cover up something." Bea became more convinced of the latter with every new revelation about Charlie Mae. "Now with poor Mrs. Feather's dead, Charlie Mae and Roosevelt are free to come out in the open with their little love fest."

The three women piled out of the car, dressed to the hilt for the wake and funeral that would follow at one of the city's better known mortuaries. The parking lot was full, forcing them to park on the street.

"I wonder if Charlie Mae will have the nerve to show up?" Hattie whispered to Bea.

"She wouldn't dare!" Bea was incredulous. "If she's as smart as she thinks she is, she'll keep a low profile. Then she and Roosevelt can slowly emerge as a couple later with some lie about how they first met." They drew closer to the front entrance, and Bea began to speak in hushed excited tones. "Just remember, you two, we're here to gather any information we can on Roosevelt and his wife. So don't waste any time." Her cohorts nodded in agreement as they went inside.

Like the funeral pro that she was, Hattie's eyes skirted her surroundings. The memorial guest book in the lobby was the first item to receive her attention. As she signed it with a phony name, her eyes searched the pages for any familiar names, but she found none. Her friends were waiting for her in the viewing room when she entered.

The room was nearly full. Most people were sitting and talking in subdued tones, while others were viewing the body and greeting the family. They spotted Roosevelt Feathers right away. He was sitting in the front row beside a darkly clad, older woman. A younger one stood at the foot of the casket talking to mourners. They guessed that the two women were Cheryl's mother Easter and her sister Sandy. They decided that Hattie would handle the sister.

The ladies moved as a group toward the front of the room and the casket. They stood together looking down at Cheryl Feathers. Long, thick eyelashes caressed her brown cheeks. Her dark hair flowed past her shoulders. She had a heart shaped face and full lips, although Hattie observed that the mortician might have enhanced them a little.

"She looks younger than the age they quoted in her obituary," Connie whispered. "And she sure was pretty. Looks like Roosevelt had it going on in that department."

Hattie's expert eye examined the casket. It was the top of the line, bronze in color, with a lining of the finest satin. The family had spared no expense.

"They could have dressed her with a little more class," Bea observed. She didn't like the pale yellow dress that adorned the body. It looked too prissy. Cheryl Feathers looked as though she had exuded class when she was alive.

They examined the flowers and plants surrounding the casket, carefully reading each card. Bea made note of one flower arrangement from S. Realty. She nudged Hattie, who alerted Connie. Confused at first, Connie studied the card long and hard before she realized that the S might stand for Schaffer.

"It couldn't be!" she whispered in surprise.

"Oh yes it could," quipped Hattie.

It was time to move on to the *real* investigating, but first—

Hattie moved to the woman standing at the foot of the casket greeting mourners. Bea and Connie went straight to Roosevelt Feathers.

"How do you do?" Hattie shook the hand of the attractive woman dressed in dark blue. A double strand of expensive pearls graced her neck. "I just want to let you know how sorry I am about Cheryl." Hattie's sentiments were sincere. She empathized with the bereaved.

"Thank you," Sandy said with gratitude, giving her a tentative smile. "And you are?"

"She was such a lovely woman," Hattie hurried on. "I know that her death will leave a void in your life."

"Yes, it will," the woman said softly.

"Well, you stay strong," she said, patting her arm sympathetically she moved on to cover the rest of the room. She and her friends had agreed in advance that the viewing room would be her territory.

Bea and Connie moved to where Roosevelt Feathers sat, but addressed the deceased's mother first. The older woman looked as if she were in shock.

"Mrs. Gaddis?" Bea knew her name from the obituary page. "I want to tell you how sorry I am about your daughter." Her heart went out to any mother who had lost a child. She knew first hand exactly how she felt.

Connie added just as sincerely, "God will get you through this."

They both shook her hand as she smiled at them in gratitude but said nothing. Then moved on to their primary prey. Bea was the first to address Roosevelt.

"And you must be Mr. Feathers." She tried hard to keep her voice steady. This was the man who might have been a factor in Frank's death. "Mrs. Feathers was a beautiful woman." That was all she could bear to say before moving away so swiftly that he had no chance to respond. Connie gave him a slight nod of acknowledgment and followed Bea down the aisle, out the door and into the lobby.

"He sure doesn't look like much," Connie noted as she and Bea stopped to huddle. "And he's not as tall as he looked in the parking lot." Bea agreed.

Sitting he didn't look like a big man. He appeared to be of average height, but he did have a muscular physique. She could see that, even though he was wearing a suit. He was a dark, berry brown in complexion, and he wore his black hair, sprinkled with hints of gray, cut close to his head. Both his nose and his mouth were broad. At best, Roosevelt Feathers could be described as an average looking man. There was certainly nothing distinctive about him. How he could attract a woman as pretty as his late wife was beyond both Bea and Connie's comprehension.

"He must be good in bed," Connie concluded.

Bea had thought the same thing. "There's no accounting for taste."

Frank had been much better looking, and she was certain that he possessed more integrity. Charlie Mae and Roosevelt certainly deserved each other.

"Okay, enough speculating." Bea rubbed her hands together rapidly. "It's time to get to work." Connie proceeded to the outside of the funeral home to cover her territory, while Bea prepared to stakeout the lobby.

The three women worked the funeral like queen bees in a hive. Their purpose was to gather as much information about the Feathers as possible and compare notes. Bea was certain that something was fishy about his wife's sudden death, especially since Charlie Mae was in the picture, and she was determined to get to the bottom of it.

Hattie settled in the midst of the mourners who sat in clusters talking in whispered tones. The woman whom she chose to sit next to was an older woman. She would guess around seventy-something. Hattie's assessment was that the woman was there to support Cheryl's mother. Whatever the case, she would know soon.

Hattie sighed dramatically. "Lord have mercy, my heart just goes out to that poor woman's family." She turned slightly in her seat toward her neighbor so that there would be no mistake as to who was being addressed. "Her husband must be heartbroken. I heard that he loved her so much."

"Uh huh," the woman answered without looking her way, but a slight shift in the woman's body language at this last statement let Hattie know that she had hit pay dirt on the first try.

The "uh huh" that had been uttered wasn't one of those that parents use when they try to appease their children by pretending that they're listening to what they are saying. It wasn't one of those "I caught you red handed" uh huhs that wives give their husbands and vice versa when they catch them doing something they know they shouldn't be doing but deny it. No, this was one of those uh huhs that said this woman knew something Hattie didn't know, and she planned on getting to the bottom of it.

The woman sat with her arms crossed tightly over her ample chest. Observing her, Hattie knew that it was going to take skill to pry the information from her. Well, skill was her middle name. Hattie poured on the charm.

"By the way, I'm Hattie Collier, and you are?"

In the lobby Bea sat on one of the brocade-covered divans talking to Maxwell Anderson. A short time after Connie had departed for her post, a kindly looking man around "sixty-something" zeroed in on her, and Bea was annoyed. He was too short for her taste, about five feet eleven. She liked them six feet and over. He had hazel eyes. She liked brown eyes, the darker the better. He wore a tan suit with a dark brown shirt and sported a tan and brown checkered tie with a matching handkerchief in his breast pocket. His Stacy Adams shoes were old school style, as were his thick and thin socks. He reminded Bea of a pimp.

After wasting her valuable time to discern whether he might be able to provide her with any information, she found out that he didn't even know the Feathers. He was there with a friend who had stopped by to offer his condolences. The two men were on their way to another affair. Bea had been trying to get rid of him for the past ten minutes, unsuccessfully. He was pestering her to death about her home telephone number, using every old line for washed up players he could think of. Now he was trying to get her cell phone number.

"I told you that I don't have a cell phone," lied Bea. She was past being annoyed by now. She was downright mad. She had tried everything to get rid of this joker, but he wasn't getting the message. Because of him she had gathered no information. "I don't believe in cell phones. I'll never get a cell phone. As a matter of fact . . . "

From the confines of her purse her cell phone began to ring. She had forgotten to turn it off. Bea pretended not to hear it. Maxwell's eyes lit up.

"Uh, your cell phone is ringing," he grinned triumphantly.

Staring him down, she looked him straight in the eye. "What cell phone?" Whoever it was could leave a message. She had a point to make.

The cell phone stopped ringing, and Bea never broke eye contact. Finally, Maxwell laughed approvingly.

"You're a tough one, Bea Bell, but I still like you." He withdrew a sterling silver card case from the inside pocket of his polyester pimp suit and handed it to her. Bea looked at him blankly. He pressed it into her hand. "Maybe you'll have a change of heart about me. I'd really like to hear from you."

He stood to leave. Winking at her flirtatiously, he walked away shaking his head and laughing, amused by Bea's resistance.

She jammed the card into her purse without a glance. It was almost time for the funeral to begin, and she had no information. What a waste of time this had been.

Outside, Connie was faring no better. She had managed to catch snatches of conversation here and there about Cheryl Feathers. From what she heard it seemed as though she had been a kind person. She did find out that her family was wealthy. The patriarch of the family had died in a job-related accident twenty years ago that resulted in a multimillion dollar settlement. Cheryl's mother had invested it well.

There was one snippet of conversation from a couple coming out of the mortuary that Connie tucked away in her memory bank to relay to her girls later.

"I thought for sure that Cheryl took swimming lessons," said one of the women as she and her companion headed toward the parking lot. "She told me once that she had taken them as a toddler at the YMCA. She's been swimming a long time. Surely she shouldn't have drowned."

"But I heard that she hit her head when the boat tipped over," her companion offered. "That knocked her unconscious. She didn't have a chance."

Connie was surprised. Bea hadn't said anything about reading that Cheryl Feathers hit her head. Maybe it was just a rumor. Then maybe it wasn't. Whether true or not, it was the only newsworthy information she had gathered by the time the funeral was scheduled to begin.

The service was a sad affair. Cheryl's mother and sister took her death hard. Roosevelt looked as though he was grieving hard as well. When he started crying and wailing over his wife's casket, Hattie whispered to Bea.

"He's probably crying cause Charlie Mae's not here."

Much to Hattie's dismay, the funeral was short. The ladies opted not to go to the cemetery. As they sat in the car watching the parade of cars line up for the trip to Cheryl Feather's final resting-place, there was a pall over the small group of amateur sleuths. Except for the rumor of the deceased hitting her head, their foray appeared to be of minimal success. That is, until Hattie made her report.

With exaggerated flair she whipped a small spiral-bound notebook out of her purse and flipped it open. Clearing her throat, she began her recitation.

"According to Mrs. Essie Faye Carson, she's known Cheryl Gaddis Feathers since she was fourteen years old. Mrs. Carson is one of Mrs. Gaddis' best friends.

"Cheryl was pregnant when she married Roosevelt, but there were complications. She lost the baby and had to have a hysterectomy. She was heartbroken, poor thing." Hattie took a moment to sympathize, then took a deep breath before continuing. "Miss Essie said that Cheryl always seemed to be making up for not being able to give Roosevelt children. She says that they seemed like a happy couple to their friends, but it was all a front. They fought a lot, and she heard that he knocked her upside her head a couple of times. She went home to her mama several times, but it was always kept hush hush because Cheryl's mother is crazy about Roosevelt. She thinks that the sun shines on him, and she took his side every time her daughter left him.

"Miss Essie suspects that Roosevelt had other women on the side, but he was slick with it. As far as Miss Essie is concerned, Roosevelt never was good enough for Cheryl."

Wetting her pointing finger, Hattie turned to her last page. "Miss Essie doesn't trust the man. She never did. She said, and I quote: 'That Roosevelt Feathers is a snake in the grass. I spotted him as being one from the beginning, and everybody knows a snake don't do nothing but crawl in the dirt,' unquote."

Hattie shut the notebook with a snap and grinned smugly. "End of report." Her friends stared at her open mouthed.

"You missed your calling," said Connie. She had to give the woman credit. When she dug for dirt, she dug deep.

"You should have been a police detective," Bea agreed. Her friend had reached new heights as a snoop.

Basking in her friends' admiration, Hattie gave a contented sigh. "Yep, they don't call me the Mistress of Meddlers for nothing."

CHAPTER 12

It was the next day that the three grandmothers met for a brainstorming session in an attempt to piece together what they began to call their *case*. Connie, who was beginning to get caught up in the intrigue and excitement of Bea's unfounded suspicions, invited the ladies to meet at her house. She set a dish of fruit and cheese on the dining room table as they gathered around comparing the evidence that had been accumulated.

"Apparently this Roosevelt Feathers and his wife put on quite the show in public," Hattie recounted. "Since we know that the two of them weren't getting along, I suppose we can assume she knew he was cheating."

Bea wasn't so sure. "We can't assume anything. But I'll bet that you're right, which wasn't a good thing for him. What if she threatened to leave him?"

"So what?" Connie inquired.

"So, that could be a reason for him to kill her," Bea stated solemnly.

"I don't know . . . " Hattie started to protest.

"Well that's my theory," Bea hurried on not wanting her conclusion protested. "Roosevelt killed Cheryl because she found out about his affair with Charlie Mae and threatened to leave him."

"Hold on, Bea." Connie was confused. "How did you come to this conclusion? You can't just make things up as you go."

Hattie hunched over her plate of fruit and cheese. "Whoo child! I'm going to have to pray for that violent streak in you. You sure got a whole lot of killing going on. First, you say that Charlie Mae killed Frank. Now you're saying that Roosevelt Feathers killed his wife. That imagination of yours is working overtime."

Insulted by her friend's comment, Bea drew herself up haughtily. "Suppose you were Roosevelt, and your wife was going to leave you. And if she did, you stood to lose everything you owned? Wouldn't you think about killing to protect your interests?"

"No, I wouldn't." Hattie was adamant.

"You know what?" Connie said excitedly. "We ought to go to Eagle Creek Reservoir where the drowning took place. Maybe we can ask around and see if there were any witnesses."

"And if there were?" Hattie inquired.

"Then if what they tell us sounds suspicious, we can get my son involved," Bea offered, impressed by Connie's idea.

"Don't the police do some kind of investigation when there's an accidental death?" asked Hattie, her brows furrowed in thought. "Look like I've seen something like that on t.v."

The three women sat looking at each other quizzically. Nobody had the answer, but Bea knew somebody who did.

"Connie, may I use your telephone?" Bea dialed

Bryant's number. Her son answered cheerily on the fourth ring. "Hi, son. I've got a question for you."

"Good morning, Mother, I'm doing fine thank you, and how are you?" His sarcasm fell on deaf ears.

"If somebody's death is suppose to be accidental, do the police investigate it before it can be called that?"

Bryant sighed patiently. "Yes, we do. It's only after the investigation that it's ruled accidental. Why do you ask?"

"Well, if you must know, Roosevelt Feathers' wife drowned."

"Yes, I heard, but what does that have to do with you or your question?" Bryant sounded suspicious.

"Just curious." Bea's tone was innocent enough, but her son didn't seem quite convinced.

"Oh yeah? It seems like you've been very *curious* about Roosevelt Feathers lately. What are you up to?"

"I was just wondering if there had been an investigation on his wife's drowning, that's all. Was it an accident or not?"

There was silence on the other end. She could hear Bryant thinking before he spoke. "Yes, there was an investigation, and the drowning was ruled an accident. As a matter of fact, the funeral was yesterday, and some of his old friends from the precinct went to it. So, tell me, Mom, what's really behind this call? This is about him and your friend Charlie Mae, isn't it?"

"Charlie Mae Shaffer is no friend of mine!" Bea bristled, and then lightened her tone. "I'm just a curious woman, that's all. Thanks for the info, son." She hung up before he could ask any more questions.

"Bryant says that her drowning death was investigated and ruled accidental," Bea reported. "But I'm almost certain that it was his police buddies who did the investigating, which means that it was probably minimal. I tell you, ladies, I've got a funny feeling about this one. I'll bet you both a million dollars that Roosevelt Feathers got away with murder."

* * * *

Connie and David looked like any romantic couple as they strolled along the path at Eagle Creek State Park. She almost felt guilty. Poor David thought the day was about spending time together. She loved spending time with him, but she also thought that an enamored couple taking a walk together would draw less attention than a single woman asking questions. Bea's suspicion about the death of the two spouses had Connie caught up in the intrigue of the whole affair. Cheryl Feathers had drowned in this park, and Connie volunteered to come to the reservoir to investigate.

The drowning had taken place near the boat dock, and that is where they were headed. As if it were an afterthought, Connie suggested that they rent a boat.

They inquired about the cost from the boat attendant, a short, balding man in his early forties. He provided the necessary information, and then Connie inquired, "I read about a drowning here a few days ago. Is it safe to go out? Do you know what happened?"

"Oh yeah, I saw the whole thing." The boat attendant seemed friendly and eager to talk as he casually leaned on a nearby boat. "It was really something. People pointing and yelling. A big commotion, don't you know?"

"And you saw it all?" Connie asked doubtfully. Her luck couldn't be this good.

"Sure did. I walked out on the pier, and there the guy

was being pulled out of the water coughing, sputtering and pointing. It took three guys to stop him from swimming back out to get the woman. I believe they said it was his wife." Shaking his head in wonder, the attendant continued, "I've never seen anything like it. It was awful when they pulled the body out. In all these years I've never seen a drowning, don't you know?"

Connie was sure she didn't know, but she said, "And that's all you saw?"

"Ain't that enough? I was telling Josh that this job is monotonous, but that sure broke up my day." He gave a chuckle but immediately broke it off with a guilty shift of his eyes.

"Who is Josh?" David asked absently. He had been ignoring their exchange but was beginning to take interest.

"Joshua Blankenship. He's here nearly everyday. He was here the day of the drowning—was just bringing his boat in when it happened."

"Is he here today?" Connie inquired.

The man pointed off to their left toward a large blond man sitting in a beach chair about twenty feet further down the dock. As they walked toward Blankenship, David gave Connie a sidelong glance.

"What are we doing? I thought we were renting a boat?

"I'm just going to ask a couple of questions. It won't take long."

David stopped. "Okay, talk to me, Connie. What's really going on?"

"You remember my friend Bea? She is really distraught over her friend's death."

"So this woman who drowned was her friend?"

"No, not exactly, uh . . . " Connie was at a loss for

words. She couldn't really explain what they were doing because she wasn't sure herself. "It's really complicated, and I don't want to say too much right now. I promise that I'll tell you everything later. Just help me here."

David studied her a moment then nodded reluctantly. They continued along the beach until they reached Blankenship.

"Mr. Blankenship?" Connie asked, hesitantly.

Steel blue eyes looked up at her, then switched to David and back again.

"Yeah? Who's asking?"

"My name is Connie Palmer, and this is David Austin. We were just talking to the gentleman at the boat rental, and he said that you were here nearly every day.

"And?"

"We were wondering if you happened to see the drowning here a few days ago?"

Slowly he scrutinized them before speaking. "Are you cops?"

"What makes you think we're cops?" David asked.

"The cops have been out here asking all kinds of questions. I just figured . . . "

"Well, there are some loose ends we would like to tie up." Connie glanced at David, daring him to contradict her.

"I told the cops everything I saw."

"I know, but could you go over it one more time in case there was something you forgot?" Trying to look official Connie opened her purse and pulled out a notebook and pen. Without looking at him directly, she said with authority, "David, would you go back to the car in case we get a call?" *All she needed was for him to blow everything.*

Shocked, David looked at her questioningly. She

returned his look with a steady one of her own that gave him no clue as to what this was about. Finally, still looking confused, David practically staggered back to the car.

Blankenship watched as he walked away, "Is he all right?"

She looked down at her pad and mumbled, "Just one doughnut too many. Shall we proceed? Can you tell me what you saw?"

Rubbing his chin and glancing skyward as though gathering his thoughts, the man recounted the drowning.

"I was docking the boat when I saw this man and woman in a canoe. I noticed them because they had stopped rowing, and I was worried they might drift into someone's path. She was leaning back against his chest, and he had his arm around her. I could hear music drifting from their radio. You know, that romantic stuff. Then suddenly it happened."

"What do you mean?"

"Like I told the other officers, it looked like her scarf blew into the water, and he was leaning over to get it. Next thing you know, the boat capsized, and they went in."

Once again Blankenship rubbed his chin in thought. "They were in the water a little while before he finally surfaced and started for shore."

"What about his wife?"

"When he did take off swimming, I guess he assumed that his wife was behind him. By then there were people out in the water trying to help. I kept looking for her, but she never surfaced. By the time I helped drag him to shore the guy was hysterical. He kept screaming to let him go. He had to go back for his wife."

Connie looked up from her note pad. "Did you see the body when they retrieved it?"

"No. I didn't stay around. It was just too much." Blankenship dropped his head.

"Thank you, Mr. Blankenship. You've been really helpful." Connie closed her pad and shook his hand.

"I hope you don't take this the wrong way, Detective Palmer, but I've never met a cop like you. You were probably one of the first female detectives on the force, huh?"

Connie turned and walked away quickly.

"Detective Palmer," he called after her, "if I remember anything else, what precinct should I call?"

Connie said nothing as she increased her speed. As she made her way back to the car she wondered how in the world she would explain this to David.

CHAPTER 13

Bea was tired. Her feet hurt, and now even her ears were hurting. The missionary society meeting had been going on for an hour, and the ladies were no closer to a final fundraiser program for their annual education drive than when they started. Bea knew the exact reason for her stress, and that reason could be summed up in two words—Charlie Mae. Thanks to that woman the missionary society was split into two factions. One wanted to continue with the annual hat show, which had been quite successful over the years. The other faction thought that Charlie Mae's suggestion of a dinner/dance was an exceptional idea.

Bea had been quiet long enough. "Madame President," she addressed Kathryn Woods, the president of the missionary society, "I don't know what you all could possibly be thinking by considering that this church body sponsor a *dance* for our fundraiser. We've given the hat show every year for the past three years, and it has been a tasteful affair."

"That's the point, Bea." Ethel Pramby was a short, pudgy woman who never had an opinion about anything until she was swept into Charlie Mae's inner circle. "I think

that the hat show is nice, but this idea sounds so elegant."
She gave a little shiver at the very thought of such an affair.

Charlie Mae took the opportunity to plead her case.
"Oh, it will be elegant! The whole affair will be formal, so
we'll have to give special consideration to where we will
have it. My suggestion would be the ballroom at the
Madame Walker Center. It's elegant, and as an interna-
tionally known cultural center, that will add just the right
touch."

"Oh p-l-e-e-a-s-e!" an exasperated Bea cried. "Am I
the only one who sees something wrong with the missionary society having a dinner and dance? This is an event
sponsored by what are supposed to be God's people."

Everyone began talking at once. The room was sheer
pandemonium. The president clapped her hands loudly
and stamped her feet in an effort to get order.

"Ladies! Please! Now, Sister Schaffer, I tend to agree
with Sister Bell. As a church organization I don't see how
we can condone a dance, much less sponsor it."

Charlie Mae stood so the group could feel the full
force of her presence. "Ladies, I know you may not
understand my position because this church is not a pro-
gressive institution. However, times have changed. We're
losing our young people to the streets with drugs, alcohol
and violence because we aren't innovative in our approach
to things. We need to lead our young people by example.
We've got to show them the way."

"By giving a dance in the name of God?" one of the
ladies asked.

Ignoring the question, Charlie Mae continued, "I
know I'm a new member, and I don't want to upset the
apple cart. Let me see if I understand the concept of the
hat show. You have captains that raise money by taking

donations from women who wear whatever color the captain was assigned. Is that it?"

Hesitantly, some of the women mumbled in the affirmative. "That's it in a nutshell," Kathryn assured her, "but there's more to it than that. The ladies donate $15 to wear their favorite color hat at a spirit-filled program that everyone really enjoys."

"The point is the hat show brings in quite a bit of money—nearly nine hundred dollars last year" one of the ladies explained.

"Nine hundred dollars?" Charlie Mae was incredulous. "This dance could net us several thousand dollars. We could sell tickets for the dinner; I estimate $50 a plate. The ballroom accommodates about 350 people. Do the math. Has the hat show ever made that much money toward scholarships? If people care to dance, we will have tasteful music from a local jazz band. I assure you, people will attend. Of course, I know many prominent people, and I'd be happy to pick up most of the tab for the dinner as a donation. That way even more of the proceeds will go for scholarships."

"Bull!" was the explosive response. All heads turned in Bea's direction. Several people gasped at the outburst, but she was on a roll. "The point is that you're full of it, Charlie Mae Schaffer. You're a big phony strutting around in your furs and riding in your chauffeured car. Everything isn't about money, and I'm tired of you flaunting yours trying to buy everybody. If we're a church, then we should act like a church, and that does not mean giving a dance and shaking our butts in the name of the Lord. It's just not right, and it's not biblical."

There was a smattering of applause and a few murmurs of "Amen!" and "Preach, Sister Bell!"

Charlie Mae eyed Bea with contempt. "I see you didn't mind shaking your butt at the class reunion when you were dancing with *my* husband."

The room got deathly quiet.

Bea ignored the insinuation of impropriety. "What I did was share a dance with an old friend. What I did not do was represent myself as a church missionary sponsoring a dance sanctioned by the church. Some may call that hypocritical, but that's my personal conviction."

"Oh, like they didn't dance in the Bible," Ethel chimed in once again. "The Good Book says, make a joyful noise unto the Lord. It also says we should praise him with the sound of the trumpet and the cymbal and *the dance*."

Glaring at Ethel until the woman nervously took her seat, Bea continued. "I know this is not my house but God's, and he welcomes all to his house. But, Lord help me, every since you set foot in this church, Charlie Mae, you've been trying to change this and change that."

Bea slowly walked over to the other woman and stopped just inches away. She raised her hand, and Charlie Mae immediately took a defensive stance that would have made any boxer proud.

"Don't get low-life on me, Charlie Mae. I just want to borrow this." Bea took the Bible that Charlie Mae had been clutching in her hand. Holding the book high above her head, she said, "Everything is *not* about money. Your husband knew that, and I'd think you would respect that since it's his money you're flaunting."

"Just what are you saying?" Charlie Mae bristled. "And what do *you* know about *my* husband?"

"I know that he was a man that didn't like deceit. Yet, he was being deceived by those closest to him." Bea flipped the book open and read the last lines of the dedication

Charlie Mae wrote to her husband. "In memory of her beloved husband, Frank Schaffer. You have my love and my loyalty always." She slammed the book closed. "You don't know what love or loyalty is." Gathering her things, Bea stalked out of the meeting leaving the women in opened-mouth silence.

The following day Connie and Hattie gathered at Bea's house, and she gave them an account of the events at the missionary meeting.

"You two should have seen Charlie Mae when I accused her of being deceitful to Frank. I admit, she kept a poker face, and did a good job of doing it, but I could tell by the way her eyes were shifting that I'd hit a nerve."

Connie laughed. "After what you did, how could you not hit a nerve?"

"I'm telling you," Bea declared adamantly, "as sure as God made little green apples, she killed Frank."

"Well if she did, you're trying your best to nail her," Connie observed.

Hattie was so shaken by the thought of a missionary society sponsoring a dinner dance she started pacing the room.

"My Lord," she fretted, wringing her hands in distress. "That woman is in the fast lane to hell, and she's going to take all of you with her."

"Actually, I don't think that the idea is *that* bad," Connie said thoughtfully. "There are a lot of people who have no trouble combining dancing with their Christianity. After all, there is a time and place for everything. It could be tastefully done."

Undaunted by the cold stares of her two less worldly friends, Connie continued, "Bea, are you sure that part of the reason that you're so upset isn't because Charlie Mae is taking over your territory. I mean, you've always headed up the scholarship drive and . . . "

"Yes, I'm upset," Bea retorted in a huff, "and with good reason. As you so incorrectly put it, that snake is not 'taking over my territory.' What I'm mad about is that she's using Frank's money to buy her way into everything including the church."

The chime of the doorbell interrupted their conversation. Still angry, Bea made her way to the front door and threw it open without checking to see who was on the other side. When she did see her visitor, she was so stunned that she could barely speak. "Charlie Mae?"

"Hello, Bea." Her greeting was cool. "You've apparently forgotten that I asked you to call me Charmaine."

Bea roused herself from her stupor. Looking beyond Charlie Mae she could see the black limousine parked at the curb. Standing outside the vehicle was a uniformed chauffeur. Her attention returned to her surprise guest.

"What do you want, Charlie Mae?"

"I'll only be a minute. After you left the missionary meeting the group voted to have the dinner and dance. Since you were so reluctant to have the event, I was appointed to chair the dance committee. I need the minutes from the previous scholarship committee meetings as well as the finance records."

Without a word, Bea stepped aside so Charlie Mae could enter. She escorted her to a chair in the living room and motioned for her to sit. "Stay here," she muttered through clenched teeth. She went into the dining area where her friends sat huddled in whispered conversation.

"What is she doing here?" asked Hattie.

"She came for the records of the scholarship committee. I can't believe they voted for this kind of fundraiser!

You better believe I'm going to have a word or two for the pastor."

Bea left the room to retrieve the records. Connie and Hattie were about to resume their conversation when they looked up to see Charlie Mae standing at the dining room entrance.

"Hello, Hattie." Charlie Mae's greeting was as cold as it had been to Bea. "I hope I'm not interrupting." Without waiting for a response, she walked up to Connie and extended a hand. "I believe I've seen you around, but we've never actually met. I'm Charmaine Schaffer, wife of the late real estate mogul, Frank Schaffer." With a slight nod Connie shook her hand.

"And I'm Connie Palmer, widow of the late real estate mogul, Robert Palmer. Nice to meet you."

Hattie let out an unladylike guffaw at Charlie Mae's stunned expression. Bea came back into the room carrying a loose-leaf binder.

"Okay, Charlie Mae. Here are the records." Bea handed them to her.

With a syrupy-sweet smile Charlie Mae grasped the binder, but she didn't follow her hostess as she started back to the front door. "I just love what you were able to do with your place! I just admire anyone who can take such a small space and make it look *almost* liveable. If it were me, I'd be so claustrophobic I'd have to move."

"Don't make me ask you to move your tail out of here," Bea hissed.

Charlie Mae looked genuinely stunned. "You've got a lot of nerve getting huffy when I'm trying to be a good Christian and hold out an olive branch. And that's after you've made unsubstantiated insinuations about my character. I've seriously considered suing you for defamation of character. But instead I thought to myself, 'Charmaine? What would Jesus do?'"

Hattie was incensed. "Don't you dare drag my Jesus into this conversation. God don't like ugly, and your actions are about as ugly as they come. You've been a snake since high school, and nothing's changed."

Charlie Mae spun around to face Hattie. "Surely you're not still upset over your husband's *high school* crush on me?"

"No I am not. He made the right choice. I'm talking about how you're manipulating Bea's church for your own ego. You have no more respect for the church than you did for your husband."

"Even if that were true," Charlie Mae responded frostily, "he was my husband to disrespect." She turned her attention back to Bea. "While you're being so righteous, don't think I don't know about your sneaking around with Frank. I heard about your little dinner meeting after the reunion."

Taken by surprise, Bea nevertheless held her ground. "For your information that was just two old friends catching up on personal things. It was perfectly innocent." When Charlie Mae gave a sarcastic grunt, she added, "I'm surprised you're acting like you care. I would think *your* friend could keep your mind off what Frank was doing."

Charlie Mae looked stunned. "I . . . I don't know what you're talking about," she stuttered.

"I think we both know *what* and *who* I'm talking about—tall, dark, and not so handsome. He probably has tear stained cheeks from missing his recently deceased wife. Ring a bell? Looks like I'm not the only one being seen in public places."

Charlie Mae clutched the binder as if to shield herself from the onslaught. She brushed past Bea as she headed for the front door, but Bea wasn't finished. "Go ahead and leave. You know I know what I'm talking about, and if I were you, I'd watch my back. Rumor has it that your cookie jar may not be the only one he has his hand in."

"I'm warning you, Bea Bell. You'd better not mess with me!" She turned to Hattie and Connie, "As for you two, I will be speaking to my lawyer about this woman's invasion of my privacy, and if you don't want to go down with your friend, you'd better watch your step."

The only thing visible to the three friends was Charlie Mae's back as she walked stiffly out the door and to her limousine. Not intimidated, Bea shouted after her, "If I were you, it's his steps I'd be watching."

Charlie Mae never broke stride. Yet, if the ladies could have seen her face, they would have feared for Roosevelt Feathers.

CHAPTER 14

When the telephone rang Bea instinctively looked at the clock. It was 4:00 p.m. on the dot. She started not to answer it. Her favorite t.v. show was coming on, and she always made sure that she was home to watch it. Her best friends knew that, so she assumed that it wasn't Hattie or Connie. They wouldn't be so rude.

With her snack in hand, she glanced at the caller ID as she passed the telephone on her way out of the kitchen. It was Dorothy Riggs calling. She knew better than to call at 4:00 p.m., too. The only possible conclusion was that it must be important, so with curiosity getting the best of her, Bea balanced her snack in one hand and grabbed the cordless telephone with the other.

"Hi, Dorothy," she greeted as she scurried into the living room prompted by the theme music from her show.

"Beeeeeeaaaaa," Dorothy drew out dramatically, "You won't believe what's going on across the street from my house."

"What?" Bea replied. From the tone of her friend's voice whatever she was about to tell her was good.

"Guess who's dressed to kill, pearls and all, and standing on the sidewalk, hands on hips, cursing like a sailor."

Bea sighed, annoyed. Why did this woman have to be such a drama queen? She'd been that way since they were kids. "Just spit it out, Dorothy, my show's on." Bea settled on the sofa and took a bite of her sandwich. The woman was wasting her time.

"All right," Dorothy sounded hurt. "If you don't want to hear how someone you and me both know and can't stand is outside cursing some man out, forget it. Goodbye."

Bea almost choked on her food. "No! Don't hang up!" She coughed and sputtered in an effort to clear her throat. *Lord, please don't let me die before I hear this!*

"Humph," Dorothy retorted, knowing that she had gotten her attention. "I don't know if I should tell you a thing, with your evil self."

"Dorothy, don't make me come over there and hurt you. Cough it up! Who is it?" Bea placed the sandwich on the table and using the remote adjusted the sound on the television.

"Charlie Mae Shaffer!" Dorothy squealed unable to hold it any longer.

"What?!" Bea turned the t.v. off. This was going to demand her undivided attention. "You're lying."

"If I'm lying, I'm dying. The heifer is out here in front of the house across the street right now cursing this man out like he done slapped her mama."

"Man? What Man?" Bea's heart rate accelerated. *It couldn't be!*

"I don't know who he is, but I think he's the one I saw helping the woman who bought the house across the street move in the other day."

"Who's the woman across the street?"

"I haven't met her yet, so I don't know her name."

"Well, describe him," Bea demanded. She listened as Dorothy described Roosevelt Feathers. This was just too juicy. "Wait a minute, let me call Hattie."

As she quickly dialed, Bea silently berated the telephone company for only being able to call one of her friends. When was technology going to invent four way? Hattie wasn't home, so informing Dorothy of the change of plans, she called Connie. As luck would have it Hattie and Miss Fanny had stopped by her house on an errand. Connie put the call on her speaker phone. This was too good for anybody to miss.

"Okay," Bea informed Dorothy, "we're all here." But Dorothy was involved in some maneuvering of her own.

"Nathaniel! Nathaniel!" The ladies could hear her shouting her husband's name. "Grab the video camera and get in here." She returned her attention to her listening audience. "I'm going to get this on tape. I've been waiting nearly fifty years to get something on her behind, now I've got it, and I'm going to enjoy every minute of it—over and over again."

She turned back to her husband who had entered the living room with the camera in hand. They could hear her instructing him to go out the back door, sneak around the front and film the action across the street from the security of a large bush in their front yard where he wouldn't be seen. "We're not having this kind of goings-on in our neighborhood," she informed him with the right amount of righteous indignation. Nathaniel tried to put up an argument, but Dorothy was adamant. He relented. "And turn up the volume," she instructed him as he proceeded to carry out her instructions.

"The Lord is gonna strike you down for being so mean," Hattie warned when Dorothy returned to the telephone.

"Well, she ought to learn to keep her hands off of other people's men," said Dorothy. She was referring not only to the former relationships of Bea and Hattie, but Charlie Mae had stolen one of her boyfriends as well when they were in high school. She wasn't privy to the information about Roosevelt shared by the other women.

"Come on, Dorothy," Bea prompted. "Time is wasting. What's happening now?"

The telephone was pressed to Dorothy's ear as she moved from the living room to the open front door and then onto the screened porch where she could see and hear better, but not be readily noticed.

"Well, they're still standing toe to toe, and the man is waving his arms around. He's saying, 'Baby! Baby! I'm telling you, she's my cousin.' He must be talking about the woman he helped move in."

"Uh huh," Hattie commented. "That lie is older than Moses."

"Now she's saying, 'That line is older than Moses, you . . .' Lord! She called him the b word."

"A female dog?" asked Connie.

"No, an out of wedlock child," Dorothy informed.

"And she stole my line," Hattie grumbled.

"Now she's calling him a liar and a cheat," said Dorothy. "Girl! She's got that finger in his face wagging it a mile a minute. I'm telling ya'll this is a lovers' quarrel if ever I've seen one. I thought her husband just died! It sure didn't take her no time to replace him."

There was dead silence on the other end of the telephone line. Dorothy was too busy with her commentary to notice.

"Uh, oh, she pushed him. Now she's calling him every name in the book. Lord, she's using names my Daddy didn't say, and everybody knows what a cursing man he was. She's turning away from him now and walking back toward her car."

"The Bentley?" asked Connie. "Is the chauffeur there?"

"No, she's driving herself in the Mercedes."

"Must be the same one..." Miss Fanny started to speak, but was hunched by her daughter-in-law hard enough to draw a protest. "What you trying to do, break my arm?"

Dorothy continued. "He's pulling her by the arm, and I mean rough, honey. She's trying to jerk away. Girl! Looks like he tightened his grip. He's pulling her toward him. He's all up in her face. 'You're not walking away from me! I'm not lying to you, and I don't like being called a liar!' She's trying to pull away. 'I don't care what you like.' Ooooooh! He looks mad now!"

"Does he look like he's going to smack her?" Bea asked eagerly.

"Close to it," Dorothy noted. "She's pushing him away. He's pulling her. Looks like they're playing tug of war. Oooooh Lord!"

"What?" The four women asked simultaneously.

"She slapped him, right across the face. It's on now!"

"Do Jesus!" Miss Fanny added.

"Oh my God!" Dorothy shrieked.

"What? What is it?" The clamor was at the point of frenzy. The women smelled blood.

"He slapped her back!"

The women all sat in stunned silence. The argument was getting out of control.

"Call 911!" Dorothy urged excitedly. "The shit done hit the fan!"

"I got it," Connie said grabbing her cell phone out of

her purse. "I don't care who it is. No man is gonna hit a woman in front of me!"

"She ain't in front of you. She's on the phone," Miss Fanny reminded her.

"No matter," said Hattie. "It's a woman thing now!"

Dorothy shouted. "Lord have mercy! Charlie Mae done took her pointed toe shoe off. Ooooh! She's going after that man like she's Muhammad Ali! I'm telling you fists are flying. Oops, there goes her pearls. Nathaniel!" she called out to her husband, "don't put that camera down. Keep shooting! The police is coming. They'll break it up. Besides, she's holding her own." She returned to the ladies. "Honey, if my man goes out there and gets involved, he's likely to get killed. That woman done gone crazy. Ya'll ought to see her. She's moving like she's forty years old. Whoever he is, I bet he won't be dumb enough to hit Charlie Mae again!"

Connie got off of her cell phone and back to Dorothy. "911 said they've gotten several calls. The police are on the way."

"Well, they better get here before she kills him. She's beating him with the heel of that shoe like there's no tomorrow. Lord! She kicked him in the nuts with that other pointy toe shoe. Them things are lethal weapons. He done fell to his knees."

"Ooooweee." The women sympathized with Roosevelt's pain.

"I hear a siren," Dorothy alerted them. "Hope its not too late. The man's holding his jewels and moaning, and Charlie Mae is beating his head with the heel of her shoe like it's a tom tom and cursing him with every hit. Ouch!"

"Any blood flying?" Bea asked, caught up in the moment.

"His! A squad car just pulled up. Lord help him, Charlie Mae done jumped on his back. She's riding him like a horse and beating him senseless screaming 'No man alive hits me!' I'm telling you, she's the devil."

"You got that right," Miss Fanny agreed, not forgetting her slight in the store parking lot weeks ago.

"The cops are getting outta the squad car and running over to them," said Dorothy. "I think the man's unconscious. He's lying on the ground. Keep rolling, Nathaniel!" Dorothy hollered to her husband, then back to the ladies, "If that fool misses this, I'll kill him. We can sell this tape to the evening news. Sure hope there's some police brutality."

"You ought to quit," Bea warned, recalling that her girlhood friend always was an entrepreneur.

"It's taking both of them cops to pull Charlie off of that man. Where she found the strength I don't know. You ought to see her—one shoe on, stockings torn, pearls done scattered every which way, dress tore and hiked up to her crotch. Girlfriends, she looks like something the cat's dragged in."

"I can't wait to see that tape." Bea didn't pretend to hide her delight. If Charlie Mae had anything to do with Frank's death, or Cheryl Feather's, it was no more than she deserved.

"Now she's screaming 'After all that I've done for you, do you think that I'm putting up with this?' The cops are pulling her away. Oh oh! She kicked the guy on the ground in the head! He's not unconscious, he's holding his balls with one hand and his head with the other. You ought to see it out here. My neighbors done brought lawn chairs out to sit around and watch. Charlie Mae is putting on a show! The cops done picked her up. They're carrying her away, and she's *still* kicking, screaming and cussing."

The four women on the other end burst into laughter at the visual image described by Dorothy. It was obvious that Charlie Mae was no wimp.

"Uh oh!" Dorothy's words stopped the laughter.

"The woman who he helped move in just pulled up. Aw, sookie, sookie now, it's really gonna get hot up in here!"

The women held their breaths. This was better than a talk show.

"The woman got out of the car. She's got them two little bad kids with her. They done been all over the neighborhood raising a ruckus. Noisiest little things you'd ever did see . . ."

"What's happening, Dorothy?" Bea growled impatiently

"Oh yeah. She's telling the police that she lives here, and she wants to know what's going on. She looks confused. The man is trying to get up off the ground, and he's gesturing toward her. The cops just got Charlie Mae in the squad car. She looks like she's about to blow a gasket. She's still cursing and going on. Done stuck her head out the window. She ain't even pretending to be a lady. She's blown my image of her for good, that's for sure."

"It was a front anyway," Bea added. "I always knew that she had a streak of alley cat in her."

"And she's sure showing it today," Hattie agreed.

"You ain't never lied," said Dorothy. "Oh my! The woman just screamed, 'What happened to my cousin?'"

"Her cousin?" the four women said in simultaneous surprise. Dorothy concurred.

"He really *is* her cousin."

" Well, what do you know," Connie observed. "Charlie Mae did all of that for nothing."

"I bet she feels like a fool." Miss Fanny shook her head at the absurdity of it all.

"The woman is helping her cousin to his feet. Girrrl! He looks like he was hit by a train. He's got to lean on her to walk. She done called them noisy brats out of the car to help her."

"Bet he's embarrassed," said Bea, "being beaten up by a woman."

"The older cop is talking to them now. They're talking low so I can't hear anything, but Nathaniel is still shooting. Sure hope he doesn't run outta tape. Maybe I can get somebody to read the man's lips. Okay, now he's pointing toward Charlie Mae. Hmmm, that older cop seems to know this man. Wouldn't that be something if they know each other?"

Again the four women on the other end remained silent. Dorothy continued.

"Shoot, I think that's going to be it. The younger cop is telling everybody to clear out and go home. Well, they can't stop Nathaniel from taping if they spot him. We're on our own property. Oh, oh! The older cop is walking back toward the squad car. Charlie Mae's sitting there like a bump on a log. She's calmed down, doggone it. It was more fun when she was acting hog wild."

"What's Ro . . . " Bea quickly corrected herself. "What's happening with the man and woman?"

"She's helping him into her car. I guess she's taking him to the hospital. They should have called the paramedics the way he looks. The older cop is talking to Charlie Mae through the window." There was a brief pause. "Okay, the woman just drove off with the man. Oh, oh!"

"Oh oh, what?" asked Connie, exasperated by the coverage. She didn't like breaks in her news reporting.

"The policeman is letting Charlie Mae out of the squad car. The man must not have pressed charges against her crazy butt."

All five women groaned at once. They had been looking forward to Charlie Mae being thrown in jail.

"Now, she's limping to her car," said Dorothy.

"Why is she limping?" Hattie asked.

"She's wearing one shoe. She broke the heel of the other one on the man's head. She's getting in her car. You ought to see her. She looks a mess. I can't wait to play that tape back. Shoot, I might even make copies and sell them. Well, that's it. She just drove off."

The disappointed sighs reverberated in all three households.

"All right, Nathaniel," Dorothy yelled to her husband. "That's it. Wrap it up!" Eagerly, he did as directed.

Before disconnecting, the ladies reviewed what had occurred. They agreed that it had been quite an experience. No one was surprised that there was another side to Charlie Mae's personality. It was a dark, vicious, sinister side that until today had not been on public display, but it left no doubt in anyone's mind that she could be deadly.

* * * *

On the Sunday following Charlie Mae's altercation with Roosevelt, Bea's church was graced with several extra guests—Connie, Hattie, Miss Fanny and Dorothy Riggs.

The four women sat with Bea waiting eagerly for the entrance of Charlie Mae Shaffer, a.k.a. Charmaine. She always arrived late at CLUCK Baptist, and the entrance was always grand. Today was no different.

Dressed impeccably as always, Charlie Mae strolled down the aisle to the second bench from the front, the territory she had staked out on her first day in attendance at the church. She didn't look any worse from her physical altercation, although Connie noted that she might have applied a touch more makeup to cover what she swore was Roosevelt's hand print across the woman's face.

After church service, Dorothy went home, disappointed that there was nothing of further interest on the saga of Charlie Mae. While an impatient Miss Fanny waited for Hattie in the car, the three friends lingered in the nearly vacant parking lot discussing their plans to get together during the coming week.

"I'm telling you, ladies, this karate class that I'm taking is wonderful," gushed Connie. "I'm learning more than how to defend myself. I'm learning self-control and self-discipline as well."

"It sounds like something that's much needed," Hattie insinuated.

"By you too," Connie snapped. She was growing tired of Hattie's less than veiled suggestions that she was on a highway straight to hell.

Bea opened her mouth to intervene when she spotted Charlie Mae headed toward the trio. She was walking full speed. She took each step with purpose, and it was obvious they were it. Connie and Hattie followed Bea's line of vision and watched with curiosity as the woman came to a stop at their tight little circle.

Bea greeted her coolly. "Charlie Mae." A knowing smile pursed her lips as she contemplated how unaware the woman was of all the things she knew about her.

Her greeting wasn't returned as Charlie Mae got right to the point. "I hear that you have some very unpleasant things to say about me to other people, Bea, so I thought I'd warn you. If you and your two flunkies don't lay off, you'll have a law suit for slander so large it will make your head spin. I hope I make myself clear."

She walked away without further ado leaving the three women stunned. They watched as she got into her chauffeur-driven Bentley and sped away.

Hattie was the first to recover as she turned to Connie. "What day did you say those karate lessons are on? It looks like we might need them."

CHAPTER 15

"This is the address according to the paper," Hattie said, folding the newspaper and placing it back in her purse.

"It looks like a four bedroom home. Why do you think Roosevelt Feathers and his wife would need such a large house?" Connie wondered aloud.

"Girl, we didn't come to appraise the house. We're doing a stake out," Bea admonished.

"You mean a break-in." Miss Fanny sat huddled in the back seat grumbling. "You three have done some dumb things, but breaking into this man's house is one of the dumbest ideas I've ever heard."

"Miss Fanny, you didn't have to come. I seem to recall you invited yourself along," Hattie reminded her.

"Somebody's got to keep you three fools out of jail," Miss Fanny shot back.

Bea, seated in the front with Connie, who was driving, turned to face Miss Fanny. "You've got it all wrong, Miss Fanny. Being the mother of a police officer I would never break the law, but I can't sit by and let two people get away with murder. What kind of Christian would I be then?"

"The kind that minds her own business," came the retort. Miss Fanny rolled her eyes.

"Hey, be quiet everybody. Somebody just pulled up in front of the house."

A tan late model sedan rolled to a stop, and two tall men got out. One was husky and looked about thirty years old. He had a football player's build and contributed to that impression by hugging a duffle bag tightly under his right arm. The other man was older looking. He walked with a slight limp as he climbed the stoop to the house.

As the front door of the house closed behind the men, the ladies began to speculate on who they might be. Before they had time to discuss the possibilities, a red convertible pulled up behind the first car. A man practically leaped from the car and hurried inside.

Hattie was confused. "I thought the point of this stake out is to figure out Roosevelt's comings and goings so we can get inside. It doesn't look like he's going anywhere tonight; everybody he knows must be coming to visit."

Miss Fanny twisted in her seat to get a better look at the house. "Figures we picked a night when he was giving a party."

"*We* didn't pick tonight," said Hattie with growing annoyance, "and it's not a party."

"How do you know?"

"You don't hear any music do you?" Hattie questioned. "Besides what kind of party is it when no women are going inside."

"Maybe Charlie Mae and the rest of them are already in there."

Hattie strained to keep her voice from rising, "Miss Fanny, there's no party, okay?"

Once again Connie urged silence as another car pulled up. Simultaneously the first two men came out of the house and drove away.

"Did you see that?" Bea asked. "That guy didn't have the duffle bag when he came out."

Connie queried her friend, "What do you think that means?"

"I'm not sure."

When yet another car pulled up to the curb, the occupants that exited this car looked unsavory. The baggy pants, gold chains and bandannas around their heads screamed gang members. The women all looked at each other.

"Are you thinking what I'm thinking?" Connie asked.

"That there's an awful lot of activity?" Bea noted.

"Roosevelt Feathers must be way more popular than I thought," Hattie added. "And he has a strange assortment of friends."

For the next hour the ladies observed the constant activity as cars and people continued to come and go.

With more than a hint of certainty in her voice, Miss Fanny said, "I bet anything these people are doing that dope thing."

"What are you talking about?" Hattie was really annoyed now. "Why do you say things out of the blue like that? What do you know about dope?"

"Hattie Mae, I'm old, not crazy. I read the paper and watch the news. I'd bet my life that's what's going on."

Bea had to admit something was amiss. "I think Miss Fanny has a point. Maybe I should call Bryant."

"And tell him what?" Connie wanted to know.

"I don't know. I'll tell him that it looks like a dope ring is being run through this house." A sudden revelation caused her to pause. "You don't think that's what Frank was referring to that time we had dinner together? Remember, I told you how he kept patting his pocket and referring to information that would stop Charlie Mae from taking him to the cleaners when he divorced her."

Her two friends were excited by the possibility. "Go ahead and call Bryant," Hattie encouraged. "Let's bust these suckers."

As Bea dialed Bryant on her cell phone, Miss Fanny squirmed in her seat.

"I've got to pee," she announced. "Connie, drive me to that gas station around the corner."

By now Hattie was furious with her mother-in-law. "We can't leave! Why do you have to go now? What if they bust these men and Charlie Mae is inside? Besides, we have to be here as witnesses for the police."

Squirming with greater urgency, Miss Fanny gave Hattie a level stare. "I can't control when I have to go. Take me to the gas station now, or I can't be responsible for the consequences."

Connie was at a loss. "Miss Fanny, please hold it a little while longer. The police will be here soon. Besides I just had my car detailed."

Bea finally got through to her son. "Bryant, this is your mother. I need you to met me on Leisure Road right away."

Picking up on the urgency in her voice he asked, "What's wrong? Why are you on Leisure Road?"

"I'm sitting in front of a house that must be the center of a major drug ring. If you come now you can catch the whole lot of them." Bea proceeded to give him the address.

"Mother, please explain to me what's going on," he

begged. "Are you in any danger?"

She assured him she was in no immediate danger and then quickly told him where she was and what they had observed. She was careful to omit the reason that they were there. She assured him she would give more details later but was adamant that he must come now.

"Are you familiar with the term 'probable cause?'" he asked. "I can't just barge into someone's home based on the fact that my mother was sitting in front of the house and noticed a bunch of people going in and out."

"Why not, sweetie?"

Bryant sighed heavily. "Try to look at it my way, even if I came—and I'm not—and I arrested someone—and I won't—I wouldn't keep my job five minutes afterward."

"What would it take to get you out here?" Bea asked benignly.

"There has to be a disturbance of some kind. Something that would cause the neighbors to complain."

"A disturbance? You're saying that there's got to be a disturbance over here before you can send the police? Any particular kind of . . . " Bea stopped abruptly when she heard the back car door slam. Miss Fanny had gotten out of the car.

"Miss Fanny, what are you doing?" Rolling down the window, Hattie called to her mother-in-law.

Without a word the older lady continued across the street. When all three women began to call after her, she turned briefly, "I told you I had to pee. When I try to hold it too long, my pressure goes up."

To their horror she marched up to the house they were watching and knocked on the front door. Hattie couldn't help but notice the feebleness she usually displayed was strangely absent.

"What is she doing?" Connie cried out.

With her hand on the door handle, Hattie wailed, "Lord, have mercy! I could never explain to Leon if something happened to his mother."

She jumped out of the car just as Miss Fanny knocked on the door. The other two ladies called after Hattie as she hurried across the street. She ignored them, intent on saving her mother-in-law.

Hattie was half way to the house when the door opened. A bald, heavyset, man dressed in jeans and a tee-shirt appeared in the doorway. Crossing his muscular arms he stared down at the old lady.

"Can I help you?"

"Yes, son, you can. I need to use your bathroom."

"What?" He asked with a half grin as he noticed another older lady rushing up behind her. "Are ya'll some of them church folks?"

By this time Hattie had reached the porch and was behind Miss Fanny, trying to lead her away.

"Come on, Miss Fanny. Let's go." Miss Fanny pulled away.

"Yes, we are church folks, but right now I got to use the bathroom. Can I come in or not?"

"No you can't. Just give me one of them books ya'll give out and leave." He held out his hand.

Miss Fanny looked at it and then back at him. "I ain't got no books. I need a toilet. What do you want me to do, use it out here?"

"Lady, I don't care what you do. Just get off my porch."

Hattie addressed the stranger, while still wrestling with Miss Fanny. "I'm sorry, mister. She's sort of confused. Alzheimers, you know."

"I ain't got no Alzheimers. I got sugar and a slight

heart murmur, but right now I gotta pee!"

The man started to close the door, but Miss Fanny stuck her foot out to prevent it. He tried to shut it anyway, and she yowled in pain.

"Ooooouch!" She squealed as Hattie tried to pull her back. "You're killing me! You're killing me!"

"What are you doing to my mother-in-law?" Hattie demanded. With increased urgency, she tried to pull Miss Fanny back again.

Startled by the old lady's painful cries, the man opened the door wider to release her foot and gently pushed her backward.

"Oh no you didn't! I know you didn't put your hands on me!" Miss Fanny stepped back and put her hands on her hips. "Young man you must not know the Lord!"

"But lady I didn't mean . . . " he stuttered in confusion.

"This woman could be your mother," Hattie admonished, "or your grandmother, and you can't expect to be long for this world because the bible says 'honor thy father and thy mother that thy days may be long upon the earth.'"

"Amen," Miss Fanny concurred. "The Lord seeth an evil doer, and he's watching you right now beating up an old lady."

"But I didn't . . . " he tried to intervene.

"I hope the Lord strikes you down right now for what you did!"

By this time the commotion at the front door had drawn the attention of the other occupants in the house. They stood behind the man in the door teasing and mocking him.

"Man, what you doin' hittin' an old lady?"

"Good thing we came up here before she kicked your ass!"

Miss Fanny wasn't impressed. Throwing her hands in the air she turned to a higher power. "Oh Lord, have mercy on these sinners."

"Yes, Lord!" Hattie closed her eyes and commenced to having a prayer intervention on the front porch. Heaven knows it was needed.

Back in the car Bea was still on the telephone with her son. Noticing the commotion on the porch, she gave a satisfied smile. "Bye, Bryant," she said disconnecting the call. She then dialed 911.

"What are you doing?" Connie asked torn between watching the action on the porch and watching the action in the car. Bea held up an index finger to stay Connie's question.

"Hello, 911? I'd like to report a disturbance." She explained that there was an assault in progress and gave the dispatcher the address. Connie looked at her knowingly.

"Why, Bea, you old fox."

* * * *

Bryant and the ladies stood across the street watching as the last of the occupants of the house was lead away in handcuffs. Bea's son was delighted.

"Do you ladies realize what this means? This is big! We swept the house, and from the look of it, this could be the largest drug bust in state history. We've arrested some major players, and there were some records found in the house that may lead up to more."

Bea smiled, pleased at her son's happiness. "We did good, huh?" She wasn't certain as to why he was so pleased, but at least he seemed to think that she and her friends had helped him in some way.

"Yes, Mother, you did good." The smile on Bryant's face faded as he grew serious. "Now that's settled. I've got a question for you. Why were you here?"

Bea looked at him innocently. "What do you mean?"

"You know what I mean." Bryant's tone grew sterner. "You don't live here. You don't know anyone around here. There's absolutely no reason for you to be in this neighborhood. It sounded like you were on a stake out when you talked to me." He noticed that the ladies avoided eye contact with him.

"I don't know about everybody else," Miss Fanny offered, "but I was looking for a place to pee. What's the world coming to when an old lady gets attacked for wanting to use the bathroom."

"Uh huh," Bryant was skeptical. "And this was the only place in this entire city where you could use the bathroom?" His question was met with silence. "And another thing, why are the three of you dressed like that?"

Bea looked at Hattie and Connie, dressed in black slacks, black sweaters and black knit caps just as she was. She turned back to her son defensively.

"We've got to justify how we dress when we go out into the streets now? I'm a grown woman. I'm way past the age when I have to explain anything to anybody about how I dress, especially my own son."

"Amen," Hattie and Connie chimed in.

Bryant eyed them suspiciously. "Does this have anything to do with the fact that this used to be Roosevelt Feather's house?"

"Use to be!" The three women spoke simultaneously.

"Yeah, used to be. When you called me, Mother, I

ran a check on the address and found out that the man we just arrested apparently bought the house from Feathers a couple of weeks ago."

"Oops." Miss Fanny gave the three women a disgusted look. "I went through all of that for nothing and still didn't get to pee."

Hattie looked at her mother-in-law askance. "What do you mean, you went 'through all of that for nothing'?"

Connie understood right away. "You caused that commotion on purpose, didn't you Miss Fanny?"

Miss Fanny winked and said, "But I still gotta pee."

CHAPTER 16

Bea smiled and stretched languidly on the sofa. She had been napping all afternoon. This was the first Sunday in a long time that she had not attended Sunday service, but she had made the decision as soon as her eyes opened. *Bea Bell, you deserve a quiet day.* Now it was mid-afternoon, and she had no plans to go to the evening service at CLUCK Baptist either. The missionary society was going full steam ahead with plans for the dinner and dance. A committee, headed by Bea, had confronted their minister with the problem, and he said he would "mull it over" and get back with them. There was to be a meeting of the missionary society after this morning's service, but Bea wanted no part. She had never run from a fight in her life, but today was not the day.

The Sunday paper slid off her stomach and onto the floor as she tried to turn on her side. She picked it up and read the same half-page article for the third time that day. She gave a slight groan when she heard the chime of the doorbell. Rising stiffly, she ambled to the door where she found Connie and their mutual granddaughter, Tina, standing on the porch.

"Grandmother!" Tina gave Bea a fierce hug and then

bounded into the house headed straight for the kitchen.

"You know where she's headed don't you?" Connie laughed as she followed Tina through the door.

"The first place she always goes." Bea nodded in agreement. "But she's in for a big surprise. I didn't cook a thing, and I'm not going to cook anything."

"You? Not cook Sunday dinner?" Connie couldn't hide her surprise. "You're not getting a big head are you just because you're the mother of a V.I.P.?"

The two friends squealed in delight at the last remark as they walked arm-in-arm toward the kitchen. They were nearly knocked over by Tina as she rushed out of the kitchen door.

"What's up, Grandmother? There's no food." She looked devastated.

The two women looked at each other and chuckled at the teenager's predicted reaction.

"Your grandmother is the mother of a star," Connie teased. "She doesn't cook anymore."

"Oh, I forgot!" Tina slapped her forehead. "Yesterday was Uncle Bryant's big day! What is he now, a captain or something?"

"No," Bea beamed proudly. "He is officially a detective. No more patrolling the streets for him." She turned to Connie. "Did you see the article in this morning's paper? I was reading it when you rang the bell."

Retrieving the newspaper, she gave it to Connie, then sent Tina into the kitchen to sample a sweet potato pie she had baked a few days ago. Brightening, Tina bounced out of the room with further orders to cut two slices for her grandmothers. The two older women sat down at the dining room table.

As Connie perused the half-page article, Bea went on

to tell them about the wonderful dinner she shared with her son and several of his friends who had taken him out to celebrate.

"And by the way," Bea added slyly, "did I mention that Bryant had a date with him last night?"

"Shut up!" Connie turned her undivided attention to her friend. "When did this happen? What did she look like? What's her name?"

"Her name is Rhonda Morgan, and she is the cutest little thing you've ever seen. She's about 5' 3", with gorgeous brown eyes. She had her hair cut in a really flattering style, and she's about Tina's size, very petite."

"But where did she come from?" Connie's curiosity was running rampant. Bryant had dated his share of women, but obviously he had been keeping this woman under wraps or Bea would have mentioned her earlier. "How did this one rate getting invited to such a special occasion?"

Bea couldn't get the grin off of her face. "I think my baby boy is finally doing some serious woman shopping. You should have seen the way they kept looking at each other. It was obvious to me that they have something special going on. She seems like a really intelligent girl, and she's from Fort Wayne of all places."

Connie couldn't believe it. "Is this a small world or what? Did you find out if she knew Frank or Charlie Mae?"

"You know I did. It turns out that a few years ago she met both of them at a charity event. She went on and on about how good looking and charming Frank was, but she thought Charlie Mae was impersonal and a little cold." Bea seemed pleased at the young woman's assessment.

Connie laughed. "I'd say the woman is very astute.

Too bad she didn't know them better. What we need is some insight into the Schaffer relationship."

Bea snapped her fingers with sudden inspiration. "You know we haven't talked to Frank's brother, Houston. He and Frank were so close growing up I can't imagine that Frank didn't share any suspicions he had about Charlie Mae. In fact, let me see if I can get Houston's telephone number."

Bea rose from the sofa and went to the telephone and dialed the directory assistance operator. After acquiring Houston Schaffer's number, she dialed. After several rings his voice greeted her warmly. Bea quickly explained that she wanted to talk and asked if they could meet sometime soon. When she hung up she turned to Connie.

"He says he's free this afternoon and to come on over. Houston's a valuable resource, and we've neglected him all this time. I'm sure he knows something."

"Possibly, but he and Charlie Mae seemed rather amicable when we saw them at the reunion," Connie cautioned.

"Maybe, but if you thought your sister-in-law murdered your brother, wouldn't that cool any friendship with her?"

"But Houston doesn't think Charlie Mae murdered Frank," Hattie noted.

Bea raised a determined brow. "He will."

Two hours later Bea arrived at the home of Houston Schaffer. When she pulled up to the sprawling new house, she rechecked the address to be sure she was at the right place. The house was spectacular. She didn't know that accountants did this well.

Driving up the winding driveway lined with neatly manicured shrubbery, she observed the front window that ran the height of the house from ground to roof. It gave an unobstructed view of the elegant front foyer and the second floor balcony. It looked as though Houston was doing well indeed. Climbing out of the car, she gave an appraising look around the affluent neighborhood that was located in the upscale Giest Reservoir area. She would have preferred to speak to Houston at a more neutral meeting ground, but he insisted that she stop by his house. Now she knew why. He wanted her to see that he was doing as well as Frank. Houston opened the front door a second after she knocked.

"Bea! You don't know how great it is to see you." He gave her a warm hug and a brotherly kiss on the cheek. "Come on in." He beckoned as he stepped aside to let her enter.

Bea couldn't help the rush of warm memories that Houston evoked. She remembered when Frank's little brother was forever tagging along with them on dates or school outings. She had never minded because Houston was always so much fun. Besides, she knew there was a special bond between the brothers, and Frank never made her feel neglected. That is, until he postponed their wedding.

"What have you been doing?" Houston's words brought Bea's attention back to him. "Did you get the thank you note for the flowers you sent to Frank's funeral."

"Yes, I did. Thank you, that was kind. I know what a loss Frank's death must have been for you. It was a loss for us all." Bea stopped abruptly as she felt the emotion rise. She did not want to cry.

Ushering her into a plant-filled great room to the right of the foyer, Houston led Bea to a chair, then left to get refreshments. The room in which she sat was tastefully decorated. The furniture was both modern and functional. Earth tones dominated the décor and gave a relaxed and soothing atmosphere. Along the east wall a large fireplace occupied nearly a third of the space. Over its long mantel hung a beautiful oil portrait of the Schaffer family. Their father, Frank Senior, was a handsome man whose commanding aura transcended the painting. Beside him, Mrs. Jeannette Schaffer struck a handsome pose. She was an exotic beauty whose keen features echoed the mix of other cultures in her bloodline. Then there were the boys, Frank Junior and Houston, approximately fifteen and ten years of age respectively. As Bea studied the painting she reflected on how much Frank's personality had matched his father and how much he looked like him. However, observing Houston staring down at her from the wall she saw something that she had never noticed before.

Bea had always known the light and playful side of Frank's brother, but this portrait was of a somber youth. The sad-eyed expression that looked back at her seemed completely foreign to the youth and the man that she knew.

"So, what's up, Bea?" Houston asked as he re-entered the room. He placed two sodas and drinking glasses on the table in front of her. "Your call suggested something other than just a social call."

"You're right, and I'll get straight to the point. How well do you know Charlie Mae?"

It was obvious Houston didn't see the question coming. He frowned, looking confused. "Charmaine? I'm not sure what you mean? She was Frank's wife for a lot of years. I know her well."

"I suppose what I'm really asking is do you trust her?"

Houston stood with his soda in hand and began to pace while pondering the question. "Of course I do. If you can't trust your loved ones, who can you trust?" He paused for a moment, then shrugged. "But what do I know? I'm hardly a good judge of character. Just ask anybody. I've had more unsatisfying relationships than you can shake a stick at. I've always been a poor decision-maker."

Bea gave him a disapproving frown. She was taken aback by the unmistakable bitterness in his words.

"I've never considered you in those terms, Houston. You could be a bit erratic in your behavior when we were younger, but you weren't that bad."

"Well, I'm glad to hear that, Bea. But if you had ever had a conversation with my mother or father, you'd know better. My shortcomings used to be a favorite topic of theirs."

"I guess I never had that conversation with them," Bea said softly. "But your life seems to have really come together, and I do trust your judgment. That's why I want your opinion of Charlie Mae."

"What is this about, Bea?"

Now it was her turn to stand. She walked behind the chair on which she had been sitting and leaned on it for support. "What would you say if I told you Frank's death might not have been from natural causes?"

The color drained from Houston's face. Bea continued. "I think he may have been murdered."

Houston's glass crashed to the floor. Bea gave a startled gasp as it shattered on the hardwood floor. For a few seconds they stood like mannequins as both stared at the shards of broken glass.

"I'll get something to clean that up," Houston offered as he hurried from the room. Bea was sure that her pronouncement was unexpected, but still she was a little disturbed by his reaction. She hadn't even told him the worst part.

After cleaning up the glass, Houston seemed to have regained his composure. He turned his full attention to Bea. "I thought you knew that Frank died of a heart attack. What makes you think he was murdered?"

"Sit down, Houston. What I'm about to say will probably shock you, so it's best if you were seated when I say it."

Houston took a seat, and Bea took a deep breath. "I know that your brother's death was determined to be from natural causes, but I believe he was killed, and I believe that I know who killed him. It was Charlie Mae."

A dead silence followed her declaration. Houston opened his mouth then quickly closed it. He bowed his head, and his body began to shake. Bea rushed to his side thinking that he was upset.

"Don't cry, Houston. It's going to be all right."

Slowly Houston raised his head, and to her surprise she saw that he was laughing, softly at first and then in loud guffaws. Bea took a step back. She was dumbfounded. The louder he laughed, the angrier she became.

"I just told you that your brother was murdered by his wife, and you sit there laughing! What the hell is your problem?"

Houston wiped tears of mirth from his eyes. "Think about it, Bea. I haven't seen you for months, and you call me out of the blue, then come here to tell me that my brother's wife murdered him. That strikes me as funny because you certainly can't be serious."

Bea was insulted. "Hear me out. I have evidence. The police will probably consider it circumstantial, but I think it's good enough to prove that Charlie Mae killed Frank."

"The police!" Houston gave her a disbelieving look. "You've actually gone to the police with this crazy story?"

Bea ignored his question since she hadn't really done so. Instead, she proceeded to explain the evidence to date.

"So you think Charmaine was cheating on Frank with this mystery lover?" Houston looked at Bea with a smirk on his face. "But why didn't she simply divorce Frank? Why would she have to kill him?"

"The great motivator—money," Bea concluded with a flare.

"I don't know," Houston hesitated. "Technically, Charmaine had money. She *was* Frank's wife, and what belonged to him belonged to her. He never denied her anything. So I'm not sure about your theory."

Undaunted, Bea tried again. "Is there really such a thing as enough money with some people? Charlie Mae is high maintenance. If she had Frank's money she wouldn't have to worry about anything."

Houston shook his head. He was not completely convinced. "When you started this conversation you asked me if I trusted Charlie Mae. The short answer is 'no.' She's a social climbing, class conscience, money grubbing phony. But a murderer...?"

Resigned to the fact that she was not convincing Houston, Bea prepared to leave. "I don't know why you can't see the truth. It doesn't sound like you get along with Charlie Mae anyway."

Houston's response made her stop in her tracks.

"I get along with her all right because I understand her. It's Frank that I really didn't understand, and I don't think he took the time to understand me."

"What are you saying?" Bea's brow furrowed disapprovingly. She didn't like what she was hearing.

"Look, I'm convinced that Frank knew he made a mistake by not marrying you. He's talked about you more than once over the years. I know that you're still in love with him, but that was the Frank of years ago. You never really got to know the real man." His comment was laced with bitterness.

"Houston! Have you lost your mind? Frank would do anything for you. It was an argument about you that led to our break up. I don't mean to imply that it was your fault. I was being selfish about our wedding plans, but Frank wanted to postpone the wedding to help you. I don't know what was going on with you, but as far as he was concerned, you came first. You were family, and that really mattered to him."

As she looked into his eyes she saw a reflection of the sadness she'd seen in the family portrait. "I'm sorry," she said. "I didn't say that to hurt you. I just wanted you to know how much Frank loved you. There's nothing for you to feel guilty about."

Houston gave her a melancholy smile. "It's too late. I already do."

After leaving Houston and returning home, Bea could not get the disturbing conversation off her mind. She was thinking about Houston's attitude toward Frank when the telephone rang. It was her son.

"Hi, Bryant. How is my favorite detective?" She beamed at the sound of her son's voice. "Me and Connie were talking about you earlier, and I was telling her what a great time I had at dinner."

"I'm glad, Mother. Thanks for coming last night."

"Like I would have stayed away. I also told her about Rhonda. She is definitely a keeper. And speaking of that, why haven't I met her before now? You two look rather serious." Bea listened carefully for her son's response.

"I haven't been keeping her from anyone. We've been . . . I mean I've been busy."

Bea translated these words to mean that he had been using the time to sort out his feelings for the young woman before introducing her to his mother. She gave him a little push. "Say, why don't you two come by for dinner tomorrow night?"

"Sorry, can't come tomorrow. I don't know what time I'll get back in town."

"Oh? You're going out of town?" Bea was disappointed. "Where?"

There was a moment of hesitation on the other end that lasted a little too long. Bea was on alert. He was hiding something. She could always tell when he was doing that.

"Up north. It's police business." There was complete silence from her end, and Bryant knew the reason. "All right, Mother. I know you'll pester me until I tell you where. I'm going to Fort Wayne. Okay? But that's all you need to know."

Bea tried not to convey her excitement. "It's something to do with Charlie Mae, isn't it? Bryant, do I have to remind you how you got where you are today?"

"Do I have to remind you that I earned my promotion? The drug raid helped, but give me a break. You and your friends didn't even know what you were doing. You were at that house by mistake—and you could have gotten seriously hurt."

"Just tell me about your trip, and I won't ask anything else," Bea cajoled.

"Fat chance," Bryant muttered under his breath, but

he did acquiesce to his mother's request. "We got a call from the Fort Wayne police. It seems the Indiana Attorney General's Office has been getting a lot of complaints about a real estate investment scam. A large number of the victims are in the Fort Wayne area."

Bea was confused. "What has that got to do with Charlie Mae?" she asked.

"Probably nothing, but your boy Roosevelt Feathers has surfaced as a suspect behind the scams. He appears to be operating with a female companion."

"I knew it!" Bea rejoiced. "The police are about to nail Charlie Mae!"

"Mother! Will you please stop it. The woman we're looking for is *not* Mrs. Schaffer. It's some woman by the name of Rosie Charles. I believe it's a classic scam. They take money from victims with no intention of investing in anything. They write checks to a few clients to make it appear that they're earning money on their investments. In reality Charles and Feathers pocket most of the money."

Bea came down from her cloud with a thud. "Rosie Charles? Are you sure? I never heard of her." Bea thought for a moment then exclaimed. "But of course, it's Charlie Mae! Rosie Charles . . . Charlie Mae, get it? Frank made it clear that Charmaine was up to something, and whatever she was plotting surely included her lover, Roosevelt Feathers. Bryant, are you sure the Fort Wayne police know what they're doing? These people are tricky."

Bryant was perturbed. "Yes, Mother, I'm sure they know what they're doing. You want to know why? Because they're trained detectives, and *you* are not. Please don't make me ask again—leave police business to the professionals."

"Yes, dear. I hear you. I'll let you go now. Goodbye."

As soon as she hung up Bea called Connie. Luckily, she was in.

"Connie, three way." Knowing that meant a conference call, Connie held while Bea connected Hattie to their call. She went over the events of the day, giving a detailed account of her conversations with Frank's brother and with her son.

"I don't understand. Anyone who knew Frank knows how he doted on his little brother," Hattie mused. "Why would Houston have that attitude toward him?"

"I don't know," Bea replied, "but I'm almost sure that this Rosie Charles thing is a ringer. I'm also sure that Charlie Mae and Roosevelt were plotting against their mates. Other than that, who is this Rosie Charles? If it's a different woman, how does she figure in with Charlie Mae and Roosevelt?"

Hattie yawned. "All I know is that we've got more questions than answers, and the Lord knows I'm too tired to do anything about it tonight."

"Yes, we'll have to get together and brainstorm on this one," Bea agreed. But one thing is certain, we need to go back to Fort Wayne."

CHAPTER 17

Less than twenty-four hours later Bea was on the road driving to Fort Wayne. Her trip was spurred by a message on her answering machine from Laura Webb, Frank's former secretary. She was familiar with the woman. She had spoken to her often when she and Frank exchanged calls. The women had gotten acquainted with each other through those calls.

Laura called to inform Bea that she had discovered a box of Frank's belongings in her trunk. She had forgotten that she put them there when she cleaned out his desk and office. Since she had neither Charlie Mae's unlisted telephone number nor a forwarding address for her, she had called Bea to ask if she might know how to get in touch with Frank's widow. Bea leaped at the opportunity that had fallen so unexpectedly into her hands. Informing Laura that she would be making a trip to Fort Wayne for business purposes, she offered to pick the box up personally. She made no false promises to get its contents to Charlie Mae, although she had every intention of doing so—*after* she went through it.

Connie went along as her driving companion. She didn't want to hear Hattie telling her how wrong it would be for her to rifle through Frank's private belongings. She knew it was wrong, but she wasn't going to let that stop her.

After getting lost a couple of times she and Connie finally found Laura Webb's house, and for the first time Bea met Laura Webb face to face. She was an attractive, impeccably groomed woman in her early fifties who seemed genuinely happy to meet her. Laura invited the ladies to eat lunch. Although anxious to open the neatly sealed box that she was given, Bea accepted the invitation, prompted by Connie who swore she was starving.

Laura's house was a spacious brick ranch. Each room was so meticulously decorated the interior looked like a page out of *House Beautiful* magazine. Their hostess served lunch on an enclosed sun room filled with well tended plants. They ate their meal of chicken and tossed salads from delicate china and drank cold tea from cut crystal goblets. They dined on a wrought iron table covered with a linen tablecloth, with matching napkins and chair pillows. It was clear that Laura Webb had an eye for detail. She was also a gracious and attentive hostess. Both Bea and Connie liked her, and conversation over lunch consisted of light banter about their respective cities.

"I don't travel much," Laura informed the ladies. "I'm basically a homebody, as you can see." She indicated her surroundings with a wave of her hand. "I haven't even been to Indianapolis that much," she said almost apologetically.

"Well this is only our second time here in Fort Wayne," said Connie. "We had no idea that it was such a nice place."

"Frank seemed to love Fort Wayne." Bea's plaintive comment was said almost as if she were speaking to herself.

"Did he?" Laura seemed surprised by the comment. "I had the impression that he couldn't wait to move back to Indianapolis. His brother, Houston, seemed to like it here better than Frank did. He was always here visiting."

"What about his wife?" Connie asked cautiously, knowing that Bea wanted to ask the same question. She had noticed that Bea and Laura had been reluctant to discuss Frank. From what she could discern, Laura was aware that the friendship between Bea and Frank was more than that of old school chums, but she avoided prying. Connie admired the woman's discretion.

"Well, Charmaine is from Fort Wayne, and from what little I know about her, she seemed loyal to her hometown."

"Yet she moved to Indy," Connie prompted. "I guess staying here after Frank's death was too much for her."

"I guess." Laura was noncommittal as she took a sip of tea.

Bea decided to try another tactic. "Tell me, Laura, are you familiar with the name Rosie Charles?"

Laura mulled over the question. "No . . . no, the name doesn't sound familiar. Is she from Fort Wayne?"

"I'm not sure, but I think she's connected to Mrs. Schaffer."

"Is she a friend or a client?"

"I don't know that either." Bea felt foolish.

"Then I can't help you. I don't know a Rosie Charles." She took another sip of tea.

Bea gave a frustrated sigh. Enough was enough. It was time to abandon discretion. She wanted some information, and she didn't plan on staying in Fort Wayne forever to get it. "Laura, what is your opinion of Charl . . . , of Mrs. Schaffer?"

Laura sat the crystal goblet on the table carefully. She toyed with the stem in contemplation before turning her attention to Bea. She chose her words carefully.

"Well, I'll tell you. I worked for Frank for the past ten years, and I really don't know the woman well. She rarely came to the office. When she did come she had very little to say to me except hello. Based on that it would be difficult for me to express an opinion about her, and Frank rarely mentioned her."

"In ten years?" Connie didn't disguise her surprise.

Laura shook her head in the affirmative. "He did speak a lot about you though." She smiled at Bea.

Bea acknowledged her smile. "You mean over the last few months?" She was touched by the thought that she had been on his mind, but Laura's next words shocked her.

"No, he spoke about you often over the years since I'd been with him."

"What?" Bea was flabbergasted. "For the past ten years?"

"Yes. He was always telling me little stories about himself and his old girlfriend. That's how he referred to you. It seemed that in his eyes you were the perfect woman."

"Well if he just said 'his old girlfriend' then how do you know it was me he was talking about?" Bea was skeptical. It beat hoping that he had never forgotten her and what they had meant to each other, then finding out that it was only wishful thinking. That would hurt too much.

"Oh, believe me, I know it was you. When he started calling you and said your name to me for the first time, I knew that you were the one."

Bea didn't question her further. Laura's last statement answered all of the questions that Bea would ever have about how Frank had felt about her. She was the one, his one and only. She would take that knowledge with her to her grave.

Their conversation continued and eventually got around to Laura's description about how she had found Frank's body. He had been sprawled on his office floor when she returned from lunch.

"His nitroglycerin tablets were still in his pocket," she said shaking her head.

Bea sat straight up. "Nitroglycerin tablets? He took nitroglycerin? I didn't know that his heart was that bad."

"I'm not surprised that he didn't tell you. Not many people knew that he took the pills. He did look the picture of health, didn't he?" Laura looked fondly reminiscent.

Bea nodded absently as she considered the information just provided. She was still thinking about it as she and Connie headed back to Indianapolis. Connie was driving as Bea sat in the passenger seat with the medium sized box perched on her lap.

"I thought that you wanted to open that." Connie nodded toward the unopened package. "That's why I'm driving."

"I will." Bea looked out of the window as she recounted Laura's words. "But I was just thinking, suppose I was wrong?"

"About what?"

"About Charlie Mae harming Frank. From what Laura said, nobody was around when she found him. Bryant reviewed the police report and told me that according to it Charlie Mae was with a client showing houses when Frank died, and I didn't know about the pills he took."

"You mean didn't take," Connie corrected, "at least

on the day he died, but now you know that it must have happened fast, and he didn't suffer."

"Thank God. But I'm thinking that maybe we've been barking up the wrong tree. If Charlie Mae had anything to do with his death, I can't figure out how she did it."

"Then maybe she didn't."

For the first time Bea had to agree. She had been so relentlessly single-minded in proving that Charlie Mae had harmed Frank that she hadn't considered the possibility that she might be wrong. It was really possible that he did die of natural causes.

Later that evening, as she sat alone in her dining room going through the box of memories Frank left behind, tears spilled down her cheeks. Instead of admitting the fact that she was jealous of what Charlie Mae had shared with Frank, she had been mean and vindictive in her pursuit of his wife as a murderer. She wasn't proud of that. She had involved her friends in her madness and at times had put them in danger in her pursuit of what she believed was the truth. Her son had tried to tell her she was wrong and she hadn't listened. God didn't like ugly, and she had shown all of her warts over the last couple of months. She hoped that she would be forgiven.

Shifting through the papers and knickknacks that had come from Frank's desk drawers, she could almost smell his cologne as she pictured him sitting behind his desk. There was nothing personal among the contents. Conspicuously absent were any pictures of him and his wife. Papers, pencils and pens all meant for business seemed to be the only things that occupied his office life.

A legal sized envelope caught Bea's attention. It appeared to have been crushed and smoothed again. She slipped it from among the array of other envelopes and documents. Opening it, she found a sheet of yellow, legal size paper that had been torn in half, then taped back together. Bea's curiosity increased.

Unfolding the sheet of paper she began to read the neatly written script:

Dearest Roo,

Our last night together was unbelievable. I reached heights I didn't know that I could climb. I can't wait until we're together again, being without you is becoming impossible. The only realistic solution is for me to get rid of Frank, and for you to get rid of Cheryl. I don't see another way out.

There were other words of endearment, but Bea didn't need to read them. She skipped to the signature at the end of the letter. *Love, Char*. For Charmaine she assumed! Her tears dried instantly, and so did all of the doubts that she had harbored. If ever there was a smoking gun, she held it in her hands right this minute.

CHAPTER 18

"Okay! Okay! We did bring Roosevelt Feathers in for questioning," Bea's son admitted reluctantly. She had been badgering him relentlessly for the past two hours until he finally gave in. "It was around three o'clock this afternoon and his attorney got to the station at 3:01, and that's all the hell I've got to say."

Bea cocked an eyebrow. She didn't care how old her children got, they were not allowed to swear around her, although she had to admit that she hadn't always held up to her own rule about the matter. However, thoroughly annoyed, Bryant ignored her look of reproach as he continued.

"This is all police business, Mother, and I really don't appreciate your trying to get involved in this."

"*Trying* to get involved. Let's not forget that if my girls and I hadn't turned you on to the affair between Roosevelt and Charlie Mae, you never would have suspected that he killed his wife."

"Allegedly killed his wife."

"Whatever. What did he say when you questioned him? Are you going to exhume Cheryl's body?"

"That's none of your business." Getting up from the

kitchen table where she had wined, dined and pumped him for information, Bryant made a move to leave. "Thanks for dinner. I've got to go."

Bea rose to follow him through the house. "He didn't give you permission to raise the body, did he?"

Bryant increased his pace as he walked toward the front door. His silence confirmed her suspicions.

"I knew it! He's not about to let the police examine that body. What about Charlie Mae? Did you bring her down to the station too?"

Her son glanced at her warily over his shoulder. "I've told you more than you need to know already."

"That means you did bring her in," Bea speculated excitedly. "Yes! Now you can nail her for killing Frank."

"Mother!" Bryant was exasperated. Grabbing the front door handle and opening it with a jerk, he turned to face his mother. "If I've told you once I've told you a thousand times, you can't go around accusing that woman of murder. You have no proof!"

"No proof! What about that letter I gave you? Now we have motive *and* opportunity. Just dig up Cheryl's coffin, and we'll keep the investigation on track at our end."

"Your end?" Chuckling, Bryant shook his head. "You don't have an *end*! Now I'm warning you, stop your meddling."

Bea drew back, insulted. "I don't know what you mean by my meddling, but you'll be changing your tune soon, I assure you. After all, I hate to remind you . . . "

"But you will." Bryant sighed.

"You bet your butt I will. You've got that detective shield that you're running around here flashing because of me and my friends *meddling*. If it wasn't for our busting that big drug ring . . . "

"And my studying for and passing the exam for detective . . ."

"Yeah, and that too, you'd still be wearing blue and walking the beat."

"You watch too much t.v. Nobody walks a beat anymore!" Too frustrated for further conversation, Bryant hurried outside. Bea was on his heels.

"Now, like I've said before, the way the girls and I see it, Roosevelt and Charlie Mae were in cahoots. First, she knocked Frank off . . ."

"Knocked off!" Bryant groaned and dropped his head.

"And then he did the same to his wife—which, obviously, you think too, or you wouldn't want to exhume the body and do an autopsy."

Bryant reached in his pocket for his car keys. Bea leaped in front of him and blocked his car door.

"Now you can't tell me that you would have brought Roosevelt Feathers—a fellow officer—in for questioning if it hadn't been for us bringing all of the information we've gathered to your attention."

Moving his mother aside effortlessly, Bryant unlocked the car door and got in, but Bea wasn't finished as she held the driver side door open.

"We're going to solve this case, Bryant." Crossing her arms in satisfaction, Bea stepped aside so that her son could close the car door. He started the engine and looked up at her as she smiled down at him smugly.

"You ladies are biting off way more than you can chew. Who do the three of you think you are anyway? Just let it go!" With tires skidding, Bryant drove away.

Bea stood looking after her beloved son. She respected and admired this younger child of hers and loved him more than she did her own life, but sometimes he could get on her last nerve, and this was one of those times.

* * * *

"After he got through insulting us, I told him that we'd see who gets the last laugh," Bea explained to Hattie and Connie as the three of them trekked along the Monon Trail walking path during their weekly exercise routine. "After all I've done for that boy, getting him promoted through our hard work and tireless efforts . . . "

"Busting that drug ring, right under his nose," said Connie with a shake of her head.

"And tracking down two adulterous murders that they probably would never have found," Hattie added.

"After all that, he's still not grateful," Bea concluded.

"Girl, that's the way it is with these kids," Hattie puffed, trying not to be the one to abandon their steady walking pace. "All they want to do sometimes is take . . . take . . . take!"

"They're spoiled rotten; that's what it is, and we're to blame for that." Connie also was struggling to keep up as she wondered what the rush could be.

"I know that James thought that the world rose and set on his boys," said Bea. "All they had to do was ask for something and they got it."

"Honey, you know that my Leon wasn't no different," Hattie reminded her friends. "If it wasn't for me, our kids wouldn't have had any discipline at all. The Bible says spare the rod, spoil the child."

The three women walked a little farther in silence, agreeing as if by mental telepathy to slow the pace a bit. Connie broke the silence.

"You know, all of the things we've been doing makes me feel like some big time crime buster."

"Well, we are good at this investigating thing," Bea reminded them without an ounce of modesty. "Shoot, we're certainly better at it than some of those make believe cops on television. Maybe we ought to form our own agency and incorporate."

"What do you mean?" asked Connie. "We're just grandmothers."

"Yeah," Bea agreed, "Grandmothers, Incorporated."

"Hey, I like that." Hattie gave a nod of approval. "Grandmothers, Incorporated. It's got a nice ring to it. I wonder if the city is going to give us a medal for busting that drug ring? After all, it was a community service, compliments of Grandmothers, Incorporated."

Bea rolled her eyes skyward. "How are we going to get any award, Hattie? Bryant said the information we gave about the drug house was filed as an anonymous tip. That way our names won't be released."

"Lord knows that I don't have any objection to that. After all, these drug types are dangerous." Hattie gave a little shiver. "I don't want them to know that I had a thing to do with costing them millions of dollars."

"Bryant said that its best we keep our mouths shut about it."

"Well, I ain't told nobody," Hattie grumbled without admitting that she had been bursting to do so. Drugs had devastated the African American community, and she felt that any success in getting rid of the problem should be noted. Bea interrupted her thoughts.

"We can't dwell on all of that right now because we've still got work to do. After Bryant left my house I called down to the police station and pretended to be a concerned relative. I found out that Roosevelt had been released."

"Do Jesus!" Hattie made a sound of disgust. "What does a person have to do to get arrested these days?"

"What about Charlie Mae?" asked Connie.

"They wouldn't tell me if they brought her in, and I know that Bryant isn't going to tell me."

"Does that mean that both of them are going to get away with murder?" There was sadness in Hattie's voice.

"Maybe Roosevelt and Charlie Mae think so, but they didn't count on Frank having friends that could unravel the web of lies and deceit that those two adulterers have spun. They probably think that they got away with everything, but they're sadly mistaken. Life has a little surprise for them in the form of three grandmothers . . . "

"With attitude," laughed Connie.

"Oh yeah!" Beah grinned at her friends. "I like that. Charlie Mae and Roosevelt are going down, and Grandmothers, Incorporated is going to be the one to do it!"

CHAPTER 19

The answer as to whether Charlie Mae Schaffer had been detained at the police station along with her lover was answered at 10:15 the next morning. Bea had just gathered her purse and was getting ready to leave the house in answer to the honk of Connie's car horn announcing her arrival. She and Hattie were joining Connie for their first karate lesson. They had decided that not only would it be good exercise, but it would also be an asset in the dangerous business of crime solving. Being prepared for trouble would only be prudent. None of them knew that trouble was about to make a dramatic appearance very soon.

Dressed in the brand new karate outfit that she had recently purchased, and that Connie called a gee, Bea looked approvingly at herself in the full-length mirror hanging in the hall. She looked good in her apparel. She especially liked the pristine white sash tied neatly at the waist. Connie had bragged that her goal in karate was to earn her black belt in a year. Bea decided that she would earn *her* black belt in six months. After all, how hard could it be learning to chop the air? Of course she would have to get to her first lesson and then find out what a black belt was and what it was for, but she was about to do that right now. Bea slipped her jacket over her gee just as Connie sounded the horn again and again and again.

"I'm coming!" Bea said aloud although she knew that the friends couldn't hear her. Grabbing her purse, she hurried to the front door and opened it. Standing before her, poised to knock on her door, was Charlie Mae Shaffer, and she looked mad as hell. Looking past her, Bea could see her girls hurrying from the car and heading up the walk. The horn had been a warning that trouble was here.

"Well, isn't this a surprise?" Bea said stepping onto the front porch. *What was this heifer doing on her doorstep— again?*

"I don't know why it should be." Charlie Mae's voice could freeze ice. "When somebody accuses me of killing my husband, I would think that you would be expecting me."

"Oh, did you say that you killed your husband?" asked Hattie. She and Connie had stepped onto the porch in time to hear Charlie Mae's statement.

"Is that a confession?" Bea deadpanned. Charlie Mae didn't react.

"So you have the nerve to admit that Houston was right about what you said?"

Bea was astonished that Houston had revealed what she had said about his sister-in-law. That was the last time she would confide in him! Charlie Mae read Bea's expression. She gave her a knowing smile.

"Oh yeah, you'd be surprised at what Houston tells me." The words were suggestive and caught all three women off guard. There was an awkward silence as Charlie Mae assessed the three friends. Her eyes narrowed.

"So this is some sort of vendetta, huh?" She looked from Bea to Hattie. "I had a little romp in the hay fifty years ago with that ugly bucktoothed man you married . . . "

"You did what?!" Hattie's eyes nearly popped out of her head.

"Now you and this tramp . . . "

"Tramp!" Bea spit back. "Listen to the pot calling the kettle black." She wanted to slap her so badly she could feel it.

"If I'm a tramp, you're one! You think I don't know that Frank was always in love with you? I knew that he planned on you two getting back together as soon as we were divorced. You were probably sleeping with him when we were together!"

"That's a lie. *I* was faithful to *my* husband."

"And Leon did not sleep with you!" Hattie insisted. "He had better taste than that!"

"Live in your dream world, Hattie," Charlie Mae sniffed. "I just hope he improved with age. As for you," she addressed Connie, "I don't know what your problem is, but I'm warning you that I'm taking no prisoners when the law suits are filed."

"Honey, you better back off," warned Connie giving her a level stare. "You don't know me."

"And you're going to become quite familiar with law very soon, Charlie Mae!" snarled Bea. "You may have had Frank cremated, but there are other ways of uncovering what you did."

"Amen!" Hattie confirmed, still upset about Charlie Mae's statement about her husband.

Charlie Mae gave a sarcastic laugh. "You're so stupid. It was Houston's idea to have Frank cremated, not mine.

Since you claim to know so much, I'm surprised that you didn't know that."

Once again the ladies were caught by surprise. Charlie Mae sensed their dilemma and turned the screws. "So I take it that you ladies based your brilliant deduction about me having murdered my husband on my having him cremated. How pathetic. My lawsuit looks better and better with each passing minute. What other dumb ideas have you three idiots come up with?"

"Watch who you're calling names," snapped Connie. She didn't like this woman at all.

"I call them like I see them," Charlie Mae shot back.

Bea wasn't about to be swayed by Charlie Mae's denials. "I'm sure that the police showed you the letter that Frank must have found?"

"Oh yes, the letter. What about it? Like I told the officers, it simply says that I planned on divorcing my husband, and Roosevelt was planning on divorcing his wife."

"Except his wife died in an accident not long after your husband suddenly dropped dead leaving you a very rich widow," Bea reminded her. "How convenient."

"Yeah, you couldn't wait to spend that insurance money," Hattie added.

"Insurance money? You think that I would risk going to jail over some paltry insurance money?" Charlie Mae turned her nose up at Hattie. "That's what I say about the poor. You have no vision. My dear, I hate to inform you, but Frank's brother received that money, and for the first time in his pitiful life he didn't squander it." She turned to Bea. "How did you like his new house? Classy, huh? I helped him pick it out." A smug smile pursed Charlie Mae's lips. "Why should I worry about some insurance money when as Frank's wife I was heir to his entire fortune. And as you know, Bea, he was a very smart man. He was also a very rich one. It was just good luck that he died before we divorced."

It was Connie's steady hand on Bea's arm that kept her from socking Charlie Mae in her mouth. "Get off of my property, Charlie Mae!" she ordered between gritted teeth. She was so angry that she could no longer look at her.

"You're going to burn in hell fire, Charlie Mae Shaffer!" Hattie huffed.

"I'll say hello to Leon when I get there."

Connie had a hard time restraining Hattie as she reached for Charlie Mae's hair. Bea helped drag Hattie into the house as she screamed, "Let me at her! Let me at her!" Charlie Mae didn't flinch as she stood looking impassively at the emotional display.

From behind the screen door, Bea addressed Charlie Mae. "Get out of here, and don't come back. Unlike you and your boyfriend, I don't welcome fights on the public streets for all the neighbors to see." This time Charlie Mae registered confusion.

"What are you talking about?"

Bea snickered triumphantly. "I'm talking about your making a fool or yourself fighting that man on the street over his *cousin* a short time back. What's the matter, Charlie Mae, don't you trust him?"

The woman's hiss was deadly. "How do you know about that? Do you have people spying on me?"

Bea smiled. "This is *my* town, Charlie Mae. There's not much that goes on of interest that I don't find out about." *Let her sweat.*

"And that includes how you helped your lover kill his

wife!" Hattie hollered over Bea's shoulder from the confines of the house. She was still seething.

Charlie Mae resumed her former stance. "You three old broads are mental cases, do you know that? I don't know where you get this stuff! Roosevelt didn't kill his wife, and I didn't help him. Furthermore, Frank Schaffer died of a heart attack. He had a bad heart. Now get that through your thick heads and get over yourselves or I might have to do something more than sue."

"I *know* that she's not threatening us." Having broken free of Connie's protective hold an outraged Hattie made her way to the opened screen door where she crowded Bea. "Say you're not that stupid, Charlie Mae."

"I don't make idle threats, Hattie, and the name is *Charmaine*."

"Your name is mud!" hissed Hattie, "and these three old broads are ready to kick ass!"

Bea and Connie both startled at their friend's uncharacteristic use of profanity. Charlie Mae had really pulled her chain.

For a moment Charlie Mae looked as if she was ready to accept the challenge of the three women glaring at her. She looked at each of them and at their karate attire, then seemed to reconsider.

Pulling up the collar of the expensive cashmere jacket she was wearing, she squared her shoulders. "The next time you see me will be in court." She walked down the steps then turned back to the ladies. "And I don't mean criminal court!"

* * * *

"She's lying through her teeth about her and Leon. I just know that he didn't sleep with that slut!" Hattie had been ranting about Charlie Mae's comment for the past two hours, much to her friends' irritation. Despite the encounter with their nemesis they had gone to their karate lesson and enjoyed it. Hattie liked the spirituality involved. Bea liked the exercise, and it was obvious that Connie liked the instructor, who unfortunately was a friend of David's. When he asked her how he was doing, her friends were curious as to who David might be. Connie made her answer simple by saying, "A friend." The ladies didn't pursue it. They had much more on their minds.

As they gathered at a soul food restaurant after their lesson, they mulled over Charlie Mae's visit.

"I'm tired of that woman coming to my house at her whim," Bea complained. "You'd think it was Union Station the way she comes in and out."

"Girl, she looked like she was ready to take us all on for a minute there," quipped Connie.

"I wish she would have tried it." Hattie was still spitting fire. "I would have turned karate into kraaaazy." She chopped the air comically, using the new hand movements that she had just learned, eliciting laughter from her friends.

"I ought to go to the police station today and get a restraining order on her behind!" Bea said between bites of crispy catfish. Swiping a napkin across her mouth, she tossed it on the table. "As a matter of fact, I think I'll do that. Here she is talking about suing me. I'll fix her little red wagon."

"Good idea." Hattie nodded her confirmation.

"What did you ladies think of what she said about Houston?" With relish, Connie licked the tangy barbecue sauce from each of her fingers, smacking her lips in appreciation.

"It sounds to me like Houston got a lot of benefits from his brother's death," Hattie observed, savoring her own plate of ribs. "Quite frankly, I'm beginning to wonder if the cow didn't tell us the truth."

Bea's brow furrowed in consternation. "The truth about what? Her having slept with Leon?"

The dart hit Hattie where it was intended. Dropping a fork full of greens on the plate, her eyes shot angry sparks at Bea. "Well, we all know that she slept with Frank, don't we?" Her chest heaved in indignation.

The atmosphere at the table was tense. Connie intervened. "If her intention was to turn friend against friend in a heartbeat, then she's accomplished her goal, huh?" Connie picked up another barbecue bone and resumed eating.

The two women got the message. Bea took a breath. "I'm sorry, Hattie. What I said was mean and unnecessary. I apologize."

Hattie deflated. "All right, apology accepted."

"I guess that I've been living with this thing for so long that I don't want to hear the slightest doubt that I might be wrong," Bea admitted. She pushed her plate away. Her appetite had suddenly vanished. "But I've got to admit that the thing with Houston is bothering me. I wondered where he got the money to live in that big house in Geist, and remember what I told you about his attitude toward Frank? It really bothered me."

"And I know that you two heard those innuendoes that she made about her and Houston," Connie reminded them. "Unless she's lying, it sounds like the two of them had a little 'roll in the hay.'"

"Now I wouldn't be surprised about *that*." Hattie folded her arms tightly.

Bea rubbed her hand across her forehead in thought. "When I went to talk to him, he said that he *understood* her..."

"Translated that means they were knocking boots," Connie said between chews.

"Knocking boots?" Hattie looked puzzled.

"That's our granddaughter's word for doing the do," Bea explained.

"Doing the do?" Hattie still had no clue.

"Having sex! Hattie! Sex!" Connie groaned in frustration.

Hattie looked around in embarrassment before returning her attention to Connie. "You don't have to tell the whole restaurant."

"Girl, you better get with the program and get busy so you'll know what's up." Connie tossed a thoroughly clean bone onto the plate. "I keep telling you that what you need to do is climb Reverend Tree's branches."

"Go to hell, Connie!" snapped Hattie. "You sound like some over the hill rapper."

"Oh, oh! That's the second time that you've cursed today. You'd better watch it or you'll be joining me down below."

"Ladies..." Bea tried to interrupt.

"I do not curse," Hattie declared emphatically. "The word hell is in the Bible."

"And what about the word *ass*?" Hattie's haughty demeanor amused Connie. "And I have heard you say the word shit over the years too."

Hattie's jaws tightened. Her eyes were mere slits as she shot sparks at Connie. "Those words are all in the Bible, you heathen! The ass shit. Look it up!"

There was a momentary beat as Hattie's words registered with the others, then the laughter began. Bea and Connie laughed until tears fell and their sides hurt. Hattie sat seething while her friends amused themselves at her expense.

"Can we get back to the subject?" Bea asked after recovering. "We need to know where Houston fits in all of this."

"I'm ready to go." Hattie threw her napkin on the table. She was still angry. "Forget Houston, Charlie Mae and their mamas! They're all going to hell." Getting up from the table, she stalked to the exit leaving Bea and Connie sitting at the table shaking their heads in continued amusement.

Hattie was standing beside Bea's car tapping her foot impatiently when they joined her on the parking lot. Still in a snit, she climbed into the back of the car without a word. They pulled off the lot and headed for home. The car remained quiet for some time until Bea finally broke the silence.

"Okay, Hattie, I'm sorry. We shouldn't have laughed at you."

"No, we shouldn't have, and I'm sorry too, especially if it hurt your feelings." Connie was still trying to hold back laughter. "But you've got to admit that it was funny."

Hattie wasn't appeased. "You two think you're so smart." She looked from one to another. "If you were that smart you'd realize that there's a car that's been following us since we left Bea's house."

"What?!" The other two women reacted simultaneously. Bea looked in the rear view window while Connie looked past Hattie out the back one.

"You're kidding!" said Bea. "Are you talking about

the car right behind us?" She strained to see the face of the driver in the mirror.

"Nope!" Hattie said with some degree of satisfaction at having upset her friends. "It's the dark car behind that one. The driver makes sure there's at least one car between us."

"How do you know the car is following us?" Connie also strained to see the car in question.

"I noticed it behind us all the way from Bea's house to our karate lesson."

"Why didn't you say something?" There was an hysterical edge in Bea's voice.

"How did I know that the driver wasn't going to the same place? Then I noticed it again when we were going to the restaurant, but I wasn't positive that it was the same car. But I'm sure now, that's the car. At least it's the same color."

"It would be quite a coincidence for the same color car to show up behind us three times," Connie noted. "Make a right up here at 38th Street, Bea, and let's see if Hattie's right."

Swerving to the right without a turn signal to warn the other cars, Bea made an abrupt turn that sent her friends tumbling in their seat belts.

"Damn, Bea!" Connie held on to the dashboard for her life. "Take it easy."

"You told me to turn!" She looked through the rear view mirror again. The second car in back of them had also made the turn. It was in the left-hand lane, far enough behind that she couldn't see the driver, but it was the same dark colored car. She couldn't discern the make or model. "You're right, Hattie. It is following us."

"I wonder why?" Connie looked worried. "Who could

it be?"

"It could be those drug dealers we busted," Hattie suggested ominously. "Maybe they found out it was us who got them put in jail."

"But we went through that anonymous hotline thing!" Bea wailed.

"I read in the papers that some of those people have connections with the Columbia mafia," Hattie continued.

"The mafia!" Bea's eyes darted back to the mirror.

"Uh uh," Hattie nodded. "The *Columbian* mafia. And I heard that them South American drug dealers don't play." The car grew quiet at that possibility.

"Well, whoever it is will have to go onto the highway if they stay in that lane," Connie said relieved. Just then the car switched to the right-hand lane.

"Aw shoot!" groaned Bea. "I'm getting onto I-65. I'm not getting shot by some Columbian mafia!" With another abrupt change of lane she drove onto the highway barely making the exit. She hated driving on the highway, but she had no choice.

"The car made the exit too," Hattie said with rising hysteria. Knowing Bea's driving abilities on the highway, she was in fear of her fate one way or the other. She whispered a quick prayer.

Connie's eyes darted toward the rearview mirror. Sure enough, the car had somehow made the exit. "Move it, Bea! Whoever is driving that car has got to be crazy!"

"Oh, Lord!" wailed Hattie. "It must be them drug runners! They might have uzis and shoot at us, just like in the movies."

"Lose him!" Connie commanded.

Bea didn't have to be told twice. Her foot hit the accelerator, and she maneuvered past cars as if she was

driving the Indy 500 Race. Lane lines didn't matter—not
that they ever did—cars, trucks, everything on wheels were
forced to get out of her way. The horn became her best
friend as she lay on it warning others to save their own
lives because she certainly planned on saving her own.

"Sweet Jesus!" cried Hattie. She started praying in
tongues.

Silently, Connie joined her as they sped past familiar
landmarks that were usually recognized from the highway
but that were currently mere blurs.

"Take the Martin Luther King to West Street exit!"
Connie directed.

Bea did. They made all of the green lights as they
sailed down the street. Connie wasn't sure that their tires
were touching the ground. Hattie's praying increased in
volume.

"I'm taking this sucker to the police station." Bea's
adrenaline was pumping. Her fear had turned into anger.
She felt like stopping the car and kicking some ass. She
was still wearing her karate outfit.

Making the arrow onto New York Street with a skid
of the tires, she turned and headed toward Pennsylvania
Avenue. A turn there would take her to Washington Street
and the city jail. Whoever was following them would regret
the day they made that choice!

Having recovered from the shock of the ride and the
fact that she lived through it, Hattie tapped Bea on the
shoulder.

"What is it, Hattie? I'm taking this fool to jail!" Bea
was excited about the possibility of nailing their stalker.

"Well you can forget that," Hattie informed her. "We
lost whoever it was a while back." Connie shook her head
in agreement.

"Yep, even a professional race car driver couldn't have kept up with you." Connie looked skyward and said aloud, "Thank you, Jesus, for letting us live to see another day."

Finding a parking place, Bea parallel parked, getting as close to the curb as she could before coming to a stop. Turning the ignition off, she gripped the wheel in an effort to steady herself. Her body was shaking. She was sweating profusely. She whispered a silent prayer of thanks of her own.

"That was close." Her trembling voice revealed the trauma of what had occurred.

"Did any of you get the car's make or model?" asked Hattie. Her friends shook their heads in the negative before she continued. "Do you think it was drug dealers?"

"I'm not sure," Bea answered with a sigh. "It was one man in a dark car. I'm sure of that."

"Charlie Mae has a dark car, and so does Roosevelt," Connie observed quietly. The words remained suspended in midair before she continued. "I didn't see the driver, but I don't think a woman would drive like that." She regretted having to make such a sexist remark, but this was no time for political correctness.

Hattie disagreed. "Bea did." The point was well taken.

"No, I'm sure it was a man," Bea stated with certainty as she took her cell phone from her purse. With shaking fingers she dialed her son's work number. "He had a hat on, but I saw the outline of a male face briefly through the mirror."

"It could have been a woman with her hair tucked under the hat." Connie wanted to consider all possibilities.

"It was a man, and I bet I know who it was." There was no room for argument in Bea's voice. Her son answered her call. "Hello, Bryant. We were just chased through the city streets like criminals. We thought it might have been drug dealers at first, but we think that more likely it was Roosevelt Feathers. You need to bring him in for questioning again. I'm going to press charges against him for stalking."

The other ladies sat in silent anticipation as Bea listened to her son's reply. She thanked him then disconnected. For a moment she stared straight ahead in reflective contemplation.

"Well, what did he say?" Connie asked eagerly.

"Is he going to bring him in?" Hattie wanted to know.

"No," Bea sighed heavily. "Bryant said that they can't get him for this because at 10:00 this morning while Charlie Mae was standing on my doorstep giving me what for, the police were arresting Roosevelt Feathers. He's in jail."

CHAPTER 20

Connie drummed her fingers on the car steering wheel as she sat in a parking lot not far from the Marion County Jail. She hated driving downtown, and going to the jail didn't add any pleasure to the trip. Hattie sat in the passenger seat gathering her things.

"Now, Hattie," an exasperated Connie began, "explain to me again what you hope to gain by talking to Roosevelt Feathers."

Hattie looked at her as though she were an imbecile. "Information, honey. We want as much information as we can get about this Rosie Charles and how she fits in with his and Charlie Mae's plot to murder Frank."

"Like he's just going to up and confess everything." Connie was incredulous.

With exaggerated patience, Hattie said, "No, but maybe we can get him to say enough to hang himself. Of course, nothing is impossible with the help of the Lord. If we pray on this matter, old Mr. Feathers may open right up."

Still skeptical, her friend asked, "Just how do you know they'll let us see him? We're not family, friends or attorneys."

"Oh, they'll let me in," came the confident answer.

Hattie held up the old, worn bible she brought along. "I come here so often, some of the prisoners think I'm an inmate." She chuckled at her own joke.

"Who do you know in jail?"

"Girl, You know I'm on the Prison Ministry at church. When Reverend Trees first formed the ministry, I knew this was an opportunity to spread the word to people who could use some hope." Hattie patted her bible then lowered her voice to a conspiratorial tone. "Reverend Trees arranged for us to see Roosevelt."

"What does that mean?"

"One of the guards, Lamont Stoner, is a member of our congregation, and he cleared it through his superior."

"Still, just the thought of being here makes me nervous. What if there's a riot and we can't get out," Connie agonized.

Giving her a critical eye, Hattie cautioned, "There ain't going to be a riot, and if you've done nothing wrong, you don't have to worry about staying here."

The two women got out of the car and reached the jail in an easy five-minute walk. Several officers greeted Hattie warmly as they passed through building security. Muffled conversations could be heard as they passed by clusters of officers, attorneys and their clients. Shackles clanked as inmates were escorted to and from the jail. Officers shouted commands to the prisoners and greetings to each other. After reaching their destination, the two women were searched, then ushered into a small room with several tables to wait for Roosevelt.

"There's usually several inmates in here at one time," Hattie informed Connie, taking pride in her knowledge. "We got lucky today."

The door opened and Roosevelt Feathers was ushered into the room flanked by two guards who pointed toward the table at which the ladies were sitting. One guard left the room. Slowly Roosevelt walked over to stand in front of the women. He stopped. His eyes shifted from one face then to the other as he tried to recall having seen them before.

Hattie was the first to break the silence. "Good afternoon, Roosevelt. Have a seat"

Ignoring the greeting, he sat across from them then frowned. "Who are you? You don't look like reporters, so why are you here?"

"The first thing I came to tell you is that God knows and sees all," said Hattie. "Even when you think you've got everybody around you fooled." She gave him a penetrating glare.

Roosevelt glared back. "*Him* I've heard of. I repeat, who are you?"

Connie spoke up. "We're investigating a crime, and because you've been arrested for it, you might want to talk to us and keep yourself off death row."

"Death row?" Roosevelt snorted. "If you two are investigators, I'm Batman." He started to rise from his seat.

"Well, Batman, I suggest you sit down and talk to us," Hattie responded.

A guard appeared behind Roosevelt and roughly pushed him back down in the chair. "You ain't the big cheese around here no more, man. When the little reverend tells you to sit, you sit."

"The what?" He scowled at the women. You two are Bible Thumpers? I didn't ask to speak to you!"

Hattie drew up haughtily. "I'm not a Bible Thumper. *I* am a missionary, and right now I'm talking to you about what you *did*."

Suddenly Hattie pushed up from her chair so violently it clattered to the floor. "Sweet Jesus!" She hollered. Connie, Roosevelt and the guard all jumped in surprise at the outburst.

"Help him, Lord!" Hattie shouted. "This man don't mean to be a sinner, but he can't help himself. He wants to do the right thing, but you know how Satan has been nipping at his heels. So help him!"

"What the hell is wrong with her?" Roosevelt demanded, visibly shaken. He looked to Connie for an answer.

She glanced at Hattie, not quite sure herself. "I think she's upset about the crime you committed. Maybe she thinks that your goose is cooked if you don't confess."

Roosevelt's eyes widened. "I want to leave. This is crazy!"

"Jesus! Let him know, Lord, that confession is good for the soul," Hattie cried out. She began to sway as she held her bible tightly to her chest. Hattie was in fervent prayer mode. "Lord, it says in your word that the truth shall set him free."

Roosevelt's eyes shifted nervously to the guard. "Man, I demand that you take me out of here!" The guard ignored him. Roosevelt shifted his attention to Connie. "You better keep this crazy woman away from me."

"Forgive him, Father! For he knows darn well what he did!" Hattie inched toward Roosevelt and was about to lay hands on him, but the guard shook his head—no physical contact. Hattie drew her hand back."

"That's right, keep away from me!" Roosevelt growled, but Hattie continued praying.

"Lord, he took a woman and led her down the path

of iniquity. He let his own lust and greed control his mind and soul."

Roosevelt looked befuddled. "What is she talking about? I never led anybody to do anything." Small beads of sweat began to form on his forehead.

Connie leaped on his statement. "So how *did* you talk her into it? Did you promise to marry her?"

"Marry her? Marry who?"

Connie leaned across the table and looked at him steadily. "Your partner in crime, that's who."

Roosevelt drew back from Connie. "Both of you are crazy!"

Connie gave him a sinister smile, just like the cops did on television. "Crazy huh? A witness saw you two pawing all over each other. You weren't even trying to hide."

Irate, Roosevelt yelled, "That's a damn lie! I never touched her. What kind of pervert do you take me for?"

Hattie stopped swaying and threw a hand heavenward. "Thank you, Jesus! The man knows he's a pervert!"

Roosevelt turned angry eyes to the guard. "Man, if you're not going to let me out of here then can't you make her shut up? She's getting on my nerves."

The guard shrugged nonchalantly then looked away. Hattie pointed an accusing finger at Roosevelt.

"Help him tell the truth, Lord! Admitting to his sin is the first step."

Desperate, Roosevelt turned back to Connie. "Okay, okay so a few people complained about what we did, but there's no way you can call it perverted. Is that why I've been singled out for prayer? You think I'm a pervert?"

"Oh, you do have problems," Connie informed him. "You commit adultery with another man's wife, then bump him off, and you think that's okay?"

Roosevelt's shoulders slumped in exasperation. "I haven't bumped off anybody! *Who* are you talking about?"

"Who are *you* talking about?" Connie wasn't sure that they were communicating.

"Rosie Charles, who do you think?"

Connie was speechless. Hattie stopped swaying. "Who! They cried in unison.

"My cousin, Rosie Charles. They've accused us of bilking a few people out of a little money using some kind of scam. You can't be put to death for that. I know! I'm an ex-cop. What kind of fool do you think I am?"

After a second of contemplation, the two women looked at each other as the same thought dawned on each. "Where does your cousin live?"

Just as they guessed, Rosie Charles was the neighbor who had moved in across the street from Dorothy Riggs. Hattie looked bewildered.

"So you were working with Charlie Mae *and* Rosie Charles?" she asked, as she tried to put the pieces together.

He looked at her nervously, fearing more religious fervor. "I don't know anybody named Charlie Mae."

He jumped when Hattie held up the bible to ward off the sin and bellowed, "You're lying!"

"We're talking about Charmaine Schaffer," Connie clarified, detecting the reason for his confusion. "We know her as Charlie Mae."

Roosevelt looked wary. "Who?"

"You heard me the first time." Connie was growing impatient. "Maybe Charlie Mae, or Charmaine as you call her, was helping you and Rosie scam people."

"What are you talking about? Charmaine has nothing to do with any of this!"

Hattie raised a brow. "I thought you didn't know her?"

"And you should." Connie gave him a knowing look. "She beat the living daylights out of you in front of your cousin's house when she thought that you were having an affair."

Roosevelt looked shocked. "How did you know about..." His eyes shifted suspiciously from Connie to Hattie. "Who are you people? What do you *really* want?"

Connie got straight to the point. "How did you and Charlie Mae commit the murder?"

Roosevelt leaped from his seat, drawing the guard's attention.

"M-m-murder?" He stammered. "What murder?" I was arrested for the investment scam, and that's it." Hattie started up again.

"Oh Lord, this heathen has gone back to his lying ways. Touch him! And quick."

"Stop that!" Roosevelt shouted, beside himself. "Guard! I'm ready to go!"

For the second time during their visit, the guard forced him to sit back down. "The little reverend *still* ain't through."

Connie motioned for Hattie to quiet down, then leaning across the table she quietly asked, "Do you deny that you murdered Charlie Mae's husband, Frank?"

Roosevelt leaned forward, looked directly into Connie's eyes and replied just as quietly, "You need therapy. I think you both are nuts. Frank Schaffer died of a heart attack. I haven't killed anyone."

"Not even your wife?" countered Connie.

Roosevelt's jaw dropped. "Now I *know* you're crazy. This visit is over." Folding his arms across his chest he refused to utter another word.

As the two ladies left the jail, they were almost at the

exit when a short, stocky man with silver hair stopped them. Taking Hattie's right hand in his, he covered it with his other hand. Connie watched dumbfounded as Hattie broke into a smile and a blush that was reminiscent of a teenager's.

"Sister Hattie. I was just going up to pay a few visits. I was hoping I'd see you today." He was obviously pleased to see her. "Did everything go okay?"

"It certainly did, Reverend Trees. We're just coming from the interview. You remember my friend, Connie Palmer."

He and Connie exchanged greetings. Still gushing, Hattie babbled on. "I'm glad we ran into you because I want to thank you and Brother Stoner for your help."

The reverend smiled broadly as he continued to hold Hattie's hand. "As I told you before, anytime I can be of help to you, you have only to ask."

Releasing her hand, he continued on his way as Hattie gave a brief wave and bid him farewell. As she did so, Connie stood back and appraised her friend. Hattie's shining hair was combed in a becoming French roll. Her face was framed by short-cut bangs. The tiny decorative pearl beads that lined the curve of the roll perfectly matched the cream-colored skirt and sweater set she wore. A dark brown cape, casually draped across her shoulders, completed the outfit. Her friend looked very nice, and it was clear that the reverend had noticed too.

"Well, well, well, look at Miss Flirt do her thing." Connie gave her a wink.

"We don't have time for your foolishness, Connie, so come on." Hattie was stone-faced as she marched toward the exit.

"I'm coming," Connie teased. "Anytime I can be of help, Sister Hattie, you have only to ask."

Hattie rolled her eyes at her as hard as she could as Connie's laughter followed her all the way to the car. They were about to drive off when Connie's cell phone rang. It was Bea.

"Are you two through talking to him? How did it go?"

"We got some interesting information. We may have to do some heavier investigating—you know, shake the trees and see what falls from the branches." She chuckled as Hatttie flashed her an angry glare.

Bea replied, "Well hurry over here. I took another look through Frank's things and discovered something we have to talk about, and you won't believe what it is."

CHAPTER 21

"Why do you think Houston lied?" Hattie asked, flipping through the date book that Bea handed her. The book had been discovered in the box containing Frank's belongings and had dominated their conversation for the past hour.

"Maybe he didn't keep his appointment with Frank. Didn't Frank's secretary say that she called Houston at home to give him the news of his brother's death?" Connie speculated.

"That's true, but she also said that when she left for lunch that day, Frank was expecting his next appointment," Bea countered.

"Did she mean Houston?" asked Hattie.

"Frank apparently didn't say who the appointment was with. Besides, the note says 'appointment with Houston – sign the contract,'" Bea read, "and from the looks of *this*, he kept that appointment."

With dramatic flare, Bea opened a folded legal-sized piece of paper that was lying on the table in front of her. It was a contract for a new car, and at the bottom were the signatures of both Frank and Houston Schaffer. The contract was dated the same day Frank died.

"Why didn't you say you had this?" Connie demanded.

"I kept trying to come up with an explanation as to why Houston lied. He told me he was in Indianapolis the day Frank died," Bea said sadly.

"Well that date doesn't lie. There is no way they signed this contract unless he was in Fort Wayne, or Frank was in Indianapolis—and we know the latter isn't true." Connie gave a shaky sigh.

Hattie was visibly shaken, "Oh Lord, please don't let what I'm thinking be true."

"You're not thinking anything that hasn't crossed my mind," Bea confessed. "We've known Houston most of our lives. This *can't* be true."

Connie looked thoughtful. "And I hate to say this, but he did stand to gain the insurance money."

"I know he wouldn't kill Frank!" Bea lamented. "Not for insurance money—not for any reason."

"People have killed for a lot less." Connie didn't want to be a pessimist but—"Think about it. As old as Houston is, his life is in such a financial mess that he needs Frank to co-sign a car loan." Connie was hit with a sudden thought. "Let me see that contract again."

Studying it for a moment she looked at Bea. "What color is Houston's new car?"

Bea shrugged. "I don't know. It wasn't in the drive-way when I went over there."

Connie's attention returned to the contract. "This contract says that the loan is for a Mercedes." She looked up at her friends. "Dark blue."

An ominous silence filled the room as they looked from one to the other.

"I don't care," Hattie wailed defiantly, "I still say it was the Columbia mafia that was following us. In the movies they all drive dark cars."

Bea denied the possibility as well. "Houston doesn't even know where I live."

"That information wouldn't be hard to find out," Connie countered. "And don't forget, Charlie Mae said that it was Houston who wanted Frank cremated when we know that Frank didn't want that."

Hattie was still not convinced. "But Frank was Houston's life line. He always looked after his brother. Houston needed him because he . . . "

"Was such a screw up!" Bea finished the sentence. "That's what he thinks of himself. At least that's what he was saying when I talked to him at his house. It was clear that he harbored feelings against Frank that I wasn't aware of."

Hattie protested. "Maybe he just met Frank, signed the contract and went back home. He was in Indianapolis when Laura called him. He loved Frank."

"Maybe he also loved what Frank had," Connie quietly stated.

"What does that mean?" asked Bea.

"Remember how Charlie Mae insinuated that there was something more than brother or sisterly love between her and Houston?"

Hattie gave a grunt of dismissal. "So what's new? She's probably slept with half of everybody she's ever met. Plus she's a liar. Remember what she said about Leon?"

"And I don't think Houston would do that to Frank," Bea added.

"The question is, would *Charlie Mae* do that to Frank," Connie said. "Houston doesn't strike me having an abundance of will power or self control."

"That's just Houston. But he does have a kind heart." Bea got up from the table to fix another pot of tea. They had been sitting in her kitchen for so long that they had depleted the first pot.

She found the conversation unsettling. What was the point of vowing to find Frank's killer if she wasn't willing to accept all possibilities? Yet she never thought his brother would be one of them. Maybe he wasn't the man she thought him to be.

Hattie looked distressed. "Connie you're more objective about this than we are, so give your take on the whole thing."

Connie rose from her chair and began to pace the room. "Suppose Charlie Mae enticed Houston for some reason."

"Vanity!" Hattie interjected.

"Yes, that could be it. Now suppose Frank found out that she was cheating. What would she stand to lose?"

"Money," Hattie repeated.

"Social standing," Bea added.

"Prestige!" Hattie said, excited by the way the case against Charlie Mae was coming together.

"Exactly. Now who else stood to gain from Frank's death?" When no one spoke, Connie answered her own question. "Houston. Suppose the two of them got together and decided they would both be better off without Frank?"

"What about Roosevelt?" Bea asked.

"I doubt if Houston knew about Roosevelt or vice versa. That doesn't strike me as information that Charlie Mae would share with either man. Besides, we can't forget that we have evidence that Houston, not Roosevelt, was there the day Frank died."

"But I told him that Charlie Mae had a lover," Bea informed her. "He got upset about it."

Connie stopped her pacing and put a finger to her

chin thoughtfully. "He might have thought that you were talking about him, not somebody else."

"Did you give him a name?"

Bea shook her head.

"Then that's probably it." Connie sat back down at the table. "So let's review what we have so far. Frank's secretary told you that she was gone a couple of hours running errands during her lunchtime. That would give Houston enough time to kill Frank and get back to Indianapolis. By the time anyone discovered Frank's body and got around to calling him, it would appear that Houston had been home the entire time. Houston really can't account for his whereabouts. He claims that he was at home sick the day Frank died."

Reluctantly, Bea affirmed the statement with a slight nod of her head. "That's true."

"So it is possible that Houston is our killer," Hattie declared sadly.

The doorbell interrupted their conversation. Bea slowly made her way to the front door, annoyed by the intrusion. To her shock and surprise the subject of their conversation was at the door—Houston Schaffer. Her heart beat wildly as she ducked, hoping he hadn't seen her peep through the small window of the door. Trying not to be heard, she hurriedly tiptoed back to the kitchen.

"My Lord, it's Houston!"

Misinterpreting the comment, Hattie gave Bea a patronizing sigh. "I thought we'd pretty much decided that."

"No! That's not what I mean. I'm telling you that Houston is at my front door."

"What!" Connie shot up from her chair.

"Oh, my God!" Hattie moved toward the telephone. "I'm calling the police."

"He knows I'm in here if he's the one that was following us. My car is parked in the driveway. What should I do?" Bea was beside herself.

"I already told you what I'm doing," Hattie said as she started to dial.

Connie gripped her hand. "Wait a minute, Hattie. We may be scaring ourselves for nothing. What are we really afraid of?"

"He's a murderer!" Hattie snapped.

"But he was your friend a minute ago," Connie reminded her.

Bea agreed. "Connie is right. We don't know if any of our deductions are true. Besides, there are three of us and one of him."

"And we know karate." Hattie calmed down.

"*I* know karate," Connie stated. "You've had one lesson. Open the door, Bea."

Huddled in a tight knot, the three shuffled to the door and peeked out the curtains. At the same moment, Houston was looking in the window and waved. With a startled yelp, the three women jumped backward.

"This is ridiculous!" Bea admitted as she freed herself loose from the group. "Let me open the door."

Hattie pushed Connie toward a seat in the living room. "Sit down and act natural," she whispered. Meanwhile Hattie took the chair closest to the phone, poised and ready to dial if necessary.

Bea opened the door. "Hello, Houston. This is a surprise. I didn't know you knew where I lived. Come on in."

Houston stepped over the threshold. Looking over his shoulder Bea saw the dark blue Mercedes parked at the curb in front of her house.

"Good evening, Bea. Ladies."

As he greeted them, the women noticed that his demeanor was quite serious. He wasn't his usual jovial self.

"Have a seat," Bea welcomed him.

"No thank you. I have something to say, and I may as well come right to the point. In fact, I'm glad I caught the three of you together because what I have to say concerns you all."

"And what might that be?" Bea asked cautiously.

"We've been friends for a long time, and I want to keep it that way. So I just want to warn you that these lies you've been spreading about my sister-in-law have got to stop."

You're warning us? About what lie?" Hattie left her chair and walked over to face Houston. She didn't like his attitude.

"Your lies about Charmaine being responsible for Frank's death."

"How do you know they are lies?" Connie stood to join her friends. They formed a semicircle around him.

"You must be Connie. I've heard about you." His tone indicated he was not pleased about what he'd heard. "Charmaine is taking your lies seriously. In fact she plans to sue you. I, on the other hand, decided to take a more direct approach. I'm asking you as a friend to back off."

"Or what?" Bea asked. She didn't like his attitude either.

"Let's hope it doesn't come to that." Houston's tone was antagonistic.

Hattie put her hands on her hips. "First Charlie Mae threatens us, and now you. Just how far does that direct approach go, Houston?"

"That's what I'm wondering." Bea walked over to the

window and looked out. "Someone in a dark car has been following us. Are you that someone?"

Houston looked smug. "From what I hear, you've made enough enemies that it could be anyone."

Hattie looked at him closely. Her eyes narrowed. "It was you! Why, Houston? Why would you do something like that?"

"He was trying to keep up with what we were doing?" Connie speculated. She was less than pleased.

Houston grunted. "Don't flatter yourselves. All I care about is the havoc you're reeking in Charmaine's life."

"Your sister-in-law is a very lucky woman," Hattie said sarcastically. "She's got *two* men who care about her well being."

Houston frowned in confusion. "What are you talking about? What two men? Frank's dead, and now there's only me."

"Think again," Connie admonished. "I see that Charlie Mae is choosy about sharing her information. You see, while you were so busy chasing after us, you should have been chasing after her because apparently she forgot to mention her lover."

"Her lover?" Houston shook his head as if scoffing her naiveté. "I hate to shock you, but *I* am her lover! Now that Frank is dead, I can confess that bit of news. So I want the three of you to back off!"

Hattie was appalled. "Houston, how could you? No matter what kind of woman Charlie Mae might be, she was still your brother's wife."

"Besides that," Bea said, not disguising the disappointment she felt at his actions, "You're wrong if you think that you're her main attraction. You're just one of her lovers."

Houston sneered at the suggestion. "You're lying."

Connie laid a hand on his arm in empathy. "She's been using you, Houston. Charlie Mae has been having an affair with a man named Roosevelt."

Houston looked at her in disbelief. "Roosevelt?"

Bea filled in the blank. "Yes, Roosevelt Feathers."

"Now I know you're lying. You'd say anything to ruin Charmaine!"

Hattie described the times that the two lovers had been seen together. "It was my mother-in-law, Miss Fanny, who saw them the first time. You can ask her. She has no reason to lie."

"I still don't believe you." His protest was weaker this time.

Bea could see in his eyes that doubts had arisen. He simply didn't want to accept the truth. She spoke gently. "You know what kind of woman Charlie Mae is. She uses people. She always has."

Houston looked bewildered as he stared past the three women and spoke aloud to himself. "She couldn't have . . . she didn't . . . " There was a catch in his voice. "I can't believe . . . " His voice trailed off.

Connie gave him a level stare. "Why did you kill Frank?"

The question hit Houston like a blow. He visibly flinched. His mouth moved, but no words came out. He gasped for air like a drowning man. Quickly he recovered but still denied the accusation. "What are you talking about?"

Connie brought him back to the question at hand. "Exactly how and why did you and Charlie Mae kill Frank?"

Houston gathered some of his former menace. "Stop saying that! Charmaine *did not* kill Frank. She had nothing to do with it."

"And why should we believe that?" Bea demanded.

Houston said nothing as the tears that had gathered in his eyes began to flow. The ladies looked at each other uneasily, not quite sure what to do or say.

"I love her," he choked. "I've always loved her." Silent tears rolled down his cheeks at the thought of her betrayal. "How could she do this to me?"

"Houston," Bea spoke in a near whisper, "how did you and Charlie Mae kill Frank?"

This time there was no defiance in his voice. "How many times do I have to say it. Charmaine did not kill Frank." Dazed, Houston turned and walked shakily into the living room, holding onto furniture for support as he did so. Then turning, he faced the ladies. His face was ashen as he gave Bea the answer she had been seeking. "I did it. I killed Frank."

Bea and Hattie still couldn't believe what he said, even after the words were uttered. Perhaps they had heard incorrectly or misunderstood the words. They stood frozen.

Houston continued. "Charmaine was nowhere around when it happened. That day I had an appointment with Frank because he was going to sign a car loan." He looked at the women with pain-filled eyes. "It was that simple. I just needed him to co-sign because my credit was a little shaky. Frank started in with the big brother speech. Would I ever get my life together? When was I going to be serious about my welfare? I was already feeling humiliated by having to come to him—again. I don't know what got into him that day, but he went on and on."

Houston stopped and let the tears flow freely. Hattie hurried to the kitchen and came back with a glass of water. She handed it to him. After taking a sip, he continued.

"I finally told Frank that I'd had it with his lecturing, and he could just go to hell. It was like he had picked up where Pop left off. Constantly yakking about my poor choices and lousy life management. Who was Frank to lecture me? He had the Midas touch all his life. I think he was on a roll from the day he was born. He was an honor student, captain of the football team, the debate team and the student body president. Hell! He was great at everything. He even took on a part-time job to help pay his college tuition. He was always Mr. Responsible." Houston's last comment was tinged with anger.

Hattie was unsympathetic. "What have you told us that is any different from what goes on in a lot of families? So you weren't the studious one or the athletic one. That's worth killing over?"

Houston gave a sardonic laugh. "You don't get it. I wanted to be like Frank. I wanted my parents to respect me like they did him. I wanted to get the grades he did. I wanted to have the business sense he did. What am I? Some nondescript accountant struggling from paycheck to paycheck. I wanted to be successful."

He turned to Bea. "I was happy for you two when he said he was engaged to you. Partly because I really liked you and partly because I knew Charmaine was hot for him. I loved Charmaine from the first time I saw her. But I was younger, and she didn't know I was alive, especially with the great Frank Schaffer around." His last words were said bitterly. Taking a deep breath, he continued.

"That day, I started to walk out of Frank's office, and he yelled at me to come back. I turned to find him leaning over his desk clutching his chest and gasping for air. I knew he had a bad heart, so I knew what was happening. He stood and began to fumble in his pocket."

"For the nitroglycerin tablets," Connie concluded.

"He was so desperate to get the bottle open that when he yanked the cap off, the pills went everywhere. They were all over the floor. He was in such pain he couldn't move."

"What were you doing all this time?" Bea asked anxiously.

Houston dropped his head. "Nothing at first. I just stood there. By the time I finally took action, it was too late. He was dead."

Bea gasped, unable to believe what she was hearing. "You just stood there and let your brother die?!"

Houston didn't answer as he avoided her eyes. "I picked up the pills, put them back in the bottle, and placed the bottle in his pocket. Then I hurried out so no one would know I'd been there."

"You could have called 911, Houston." Hattie's voice was filled with sadness.

"I didn't want anyone to know that I was there. I figured people would question why I didn't help him with his medicine. It had to be murder, my not helping. I panicked. I thought that if there was an autopsy, the coroner would know that he hadn't died right away."

"So you had his body cremated so there could never be an autopsy," Connie summarized. A tearful Houston nodded.

For several minutes no one spoke. The deafening silence underscored the anguish of Houston's revelation.

In a choked whisper Bea asked, "Why, Houston? Why?"

"I don't know," came Houston's tortured cry. "I guess I started thinking about how he had been berating me. How he had everything. How he never had to work for anything—at least not like me. All I ever did was mess up. I remembered how our parents always talked him up and then mentioned me as an afterthought. Then I thought of Charmaine."

"What about her?" Hattie sounded angry.

Houston's eyes seemed to beg for understanding. "I-I-I don't know. The things she said to me and did to me. I thought she loved me, and in the back of my mind I thought this might be my chance to . . . " Houston couldn't continue. His shoulders shook as sobs racked his body.

"Let it go, Houston," a compassionate Connie urged. In spite of his troubling revelation, she couldn't help but feel sorry for him. It was difficult understanding his warped conclusions about his family dynamics, but he was a man in pain.

Shaking her head sadly, Hattie put her head in her hand, "Oh Lord, help him."

Bea stirred from her stupor. Her sympathy for Houston was not as pronounced as Connie's. "You stood there like a coward and let him die." The words ripped through her heart like a jagged knife as she shed her own silent tears.

She was on an emotional roller coaster. She wanted to hate Houston. After all, she was looking at the man responsible for the death of Frank Shaffer, a man she had loved most of her life. Yet, somehow she felt sympathetic toward him, and that didn't fare well with her.

Bea had done what she started out to do. As promised, she had found Frank's killer. The question now was what to do next. It had to be the right thing. Reaching out, she patted his shaking shoulder.

"Everything will be all right, Houston. Everything will be fine." She made a move toward the telephone, but Houston grabbed her arm as she passed him.

"What are you going to do?" He sounded desperate.

Bea looked down at the grip he had on her arm and gave his hand a reassuring pat. "I'm going to call my son, Bryant. He's a detective with the police department. Once he hears your story, I believe he can help you."

Houston nodded. Releasing her, he drew his hand across his eyes, wiping away the tears. With a heavy heart, Bea went to the telephone to dial her son's telephone number. Meanwhile, Hattie had another suggestion.

"You need to pray, Houston. We can pray with you."

Rising, Houston gave Hattie a haunted smile. "You can pray for me, Hattie, but I don't think anyone will hear you. I may be beyond prayer. Right now, I just need to be alone.

"You can't run from this, Houston," Bea advised as Houston opened the front door to leave.

He gave a heavy sigh. "I know, Bea. I've been trying to do that since the day Frank died."

EPILOGUE

"Solving crime is a lot harder than it looks on television," Hattie commented between bites of the steak Bea's son had prepared for his mother and her friends at her request. He seldom passed up the chance to show off his culinary skills. It was greatly appreciated, and everybody at the table ate heartily.

Bryant laughed. "Solving crime? Is that what you ladies think you were doing."

"Excuse me?" Bea was insulted. "We *were* solving crime, and we did quite well, thank you."

Connie agreed. "Tell me the streets of Indianapolis aren't safer because of us?"

The three women laughed gleefully and gave each other high-fives.

"I really do feel sorry for Houston though," Connie continued. "He seems like such a nice guy. It's too bad he didn't talk out his feelings with his parents and brother years ago."

"What will happen to him now?" Hattie asked.

"Well, we'll have to wait until after the Grand Jury convenes to find out what his fate will be," Bryant answered. "He may have to stand trial. Then again, maybe he won't. We'll see."

"But there has got to be some price to pay for standing by while his brother was dying!" Bea still vacillated between anger with Houston and pity for him whenever she thought about his actions.

"I think having to face the Lord on Judgement Day knowing what he did will be the biggest price he'll have to pay," Hattie said somberly. "And having to live each day with that on his conscience is a heavy price as well."

"No doubt," Bryant sighed. "But getting back to you ladies, I want you to understand that investigating crime is serious business. I don't want you doing this kind of thing again, and I mean it. You three could have gotten hurt—or worse."

"It should be obvious that we know how to take care of ourselves," Hattie gloated. "Think about it! Thanks to us you caught two scam artists . . . "

"By accident," Bryant chuckled.

"Five drug dealers," Connie added.

"Because Ms. Fanny had to go to the bathroom," he reminded them.

"And you had two killers exposed," Bea stated smugly.

Bryant choked on the steak he was eating. "Two killers! Houston—who didn't exactly kill his brother—and who else?"

"If you had exhumed Cheryl Feathers' body like we said, you'd have a murderer behind bars instead of a swindler," Hattie declared haughtily.

Bryant let out an exasperated sigh. "Ladies, Cheryl Feathers drowned. It was an accident. Case closed. Do I have to remind you that there were witnesses?"

As Bryant and the ladies loudly debated the issue, a gaunt man suddenly appeared from the side of the house and ambled toward the picnic table in the backyard where they were seated.

Bryant noticed him first. "Can I help you?"

Smiling the man advanced toward them. "I heard your voices back here. I really didn't mean to interrupt. Looks like you're having quite a celebration going on back here." They looked at him expectantly. He continued, "Actually, I'm looking for a Mrs. Beatrice Bell?"

"I'm Beatrice Bell," she spoke up. "What can I do for you, Mr. . . . ?"

Still smiling, the man held out his hand appearing to offer a handshake. Instead he slapped a piece of paper in Bea's hand.

"Consider yourself served," he announced and then quickly turned and hurried from the yard.

Bea stood dumbfounded as she stared at the paper. "What in the world?"

Bryant took the paper from her hand while the other ladies gathered around him straining to see what he was reading.

"I knew this would happen," he said after scanning the document. "You're being sued by Mrs. Charmaine Schaffer."

"What?" cried Bea. "That heifer!" Snatching the paper from Bryant she read it for herself.

"What is she suing for?" Connie wanted to know.

"Something about slander and malicious intent," Bea sputtered. "And after all we did for her!"

"Say what?" Bryant was flabbergasted.

"For one thing, we got her away from that snake, Roosevelt Feathers," his mother answered piously, slamming the paper on the table with disdain. "He might have swindled her out of every dime Frank left her if not for us."

Bea fumed as she read the summons again. In an effort to console her friend, Hattie gently patted her on the arm.

"And after she spread that filthy lie about her and Leon, we didn't stoop to spreading the word that she was an adulterous tramp," Hattie said indignantly. She added, "Don't worry, Bea. Connie and me are behind you one hundred percent."

Bea looked at her two cohorts. "No, actually you're *beside* me one hundred percent."

"What do you mean?" Connie frowned.

"She named all three of us in the suit," Bea informed them.

"Hell no!" Now it was Connie's turn to jump from her seat. "She's messing with the wrong sister now!"

Hattie was livid, "If I wasn't a Christian, I'd go over there and kick the snot out of her."

"But you *are* Christians!" Bryant saw the need to take control. "I assume that means you will handle this through the courts like ladies."

Bea fought to control her temper. "Humph! I'll let it go for now." She folded the summons and put it in her pocket.

"Well, it looks like we're going to have a lot to do before our trip to Memphis," Connie concluded.

"Memphis?" Bryant looked at Bea and raised a questioning brow. "Why are you going to Memphis? Another case?" He snickered at his own joke.

Bea avoided his eyes. When she didn't answer, he was immediately suspicious. Taking her by the shoulders Bryant made her look him in the eyes.

"Mother, please tell me that there will be no repeat

performance of your last so-called case. Promise me that you will leave detective work to the professionals."

Bea looked at her son and smiled mischievously. "I love you, son, but you know me. I never make a promise I can't keep."

THE END

AUTHOR BIOGRAPHIES

L. Barnett Evans is a novelist, playwright and award-winning storyteller who regularly appears in libraries and schools and various other venues across the country. Her first novel, *And All the People Said...* is a romantic/suspense thriller. She has written several feature articles for newspaper and magazine publications. As a playwright her works include the Christian-oriented plays *Is God Calling my Name?*, *North Star*, and *The Body of Christ*. Through her company, Skye Writing Enterprises, she is available as a speaker and workshop facilitator. She holds a BA degree in Business Administration from Indiana Institute of Technology. She is a native of Indianapolis, Indiana where she lives with her youngest of two children and works in the area of human resources. *Grandmothers, Incorporated* is her first collaborative effort. Visit Evans' web site at:

www.lillieevans.com.

Crystal Rhodes is a novelist, as well as an award-winning playwright. Her plays have been produced in theatres across the United States. Her first novel, *Sin* received critical acclaim and her second novel *Sweet Sacrifice* was nominated for the Romance in Color Reviewer's Choice Award as Romance Suspense Book of the Year. Rhodes has written for newspapers, magazines and television. She holds a B.A. degree in social work from Indiana University and a M.A. degree in Sociology from Atlanta University. Look for the release of her next novel *Small Sensations* and visit her web site at:

www.crystalrhodes.com.